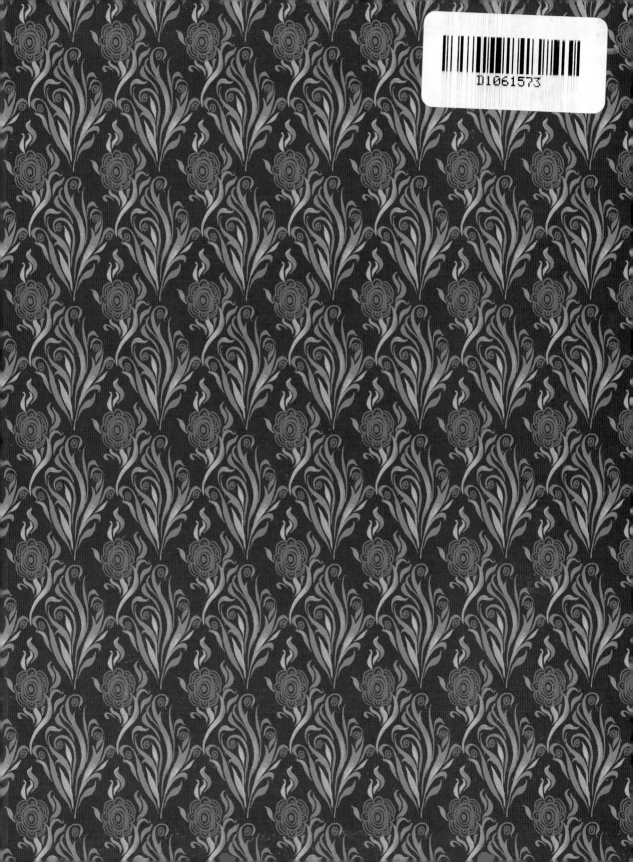

PHILOMEL BOOKS
An imprint of Penguin Random House LLC, New York

First published in Spain by Penguin Random House Grupo Editorial in 2018.
First published in the United States of America by Philomel,
an imprint of Penguin Random House LLC, 2020.

Visit us online at penguinrandomhouse.com

Philomel Books is a registered trademark of Penguin Random House LLC.

LIBRARY OF CONGRESS CATALOGING-IN-PUBLICATION DATA
Names: Sayalero, Myriam, author. | Torrent, Dani, 1974–illustrator. | Unger, David, translator.
Title: Folktales for fearless girls : the stories we were never told / written by Myriam Sayalero; illustrated by Dani Torrent ; translated by David Unger. Other titles: Quentos que nunca nos contaron. English Description: New York : Philomel Books, 2020. | "Originally published in Spain by Penguin Random House Grupo Editorial in 2018." | Audience: Ages 8–12. | Audience: Grades 4–6. | Summary: "A collection of folktales from around the world in which girls and women save the day"— Provided by publisher. Identifiers: LCCN 2019030848 (print) | LCCN 2019030849 (ebook) | ISBN 9780593115220 (hardcover) | ISBN 9780593115237 (kindle edition) | ISBN 9780593115244 (epub) | Subjects: LCSH: Tales. | CYAC: Folklore. Classification: LCC PZ8.1.S272 Fol 2020 (print) | LCC PZ8.1.S272 (ebook) | DDC 398.2 [E]—dc23
LC record available at https://lccn.loc.gov/2019030848
LC ebook record available at https://lccn.loc.gov/2019030849

Manufactured in China.

ISBN 9780593115220

10 9 8 7 6 5 4 3 2 1

Edited by Talia Benamy.
Design by Ellice M. Lee.
Text set in ITC Usherwood Std.

FOLKTALES for FEARLESS GIRLS

· THE STORIES WE WERE NEVER TOLD ·

Written by
Myriam Sayalero

Illustrated by
Dani Torrent

Translated by
David Unger

PHILOMEL BOOKS

CONTENTS

Introduction

Walter Scott's *The Talisman* is the first book I ever remember reading. I read that gorgeous hardcover illustrated edition repeatedly, until a new book— Jules Verne's *Michael Strogoff*—fell into my hands. I think both books were part of the same collection. Later, I read *Ivanhoe*, along with dozens of other books whose names I no longer remember.

I lived in these stories while reading them: through them, I traveled to far-off countries and galloped across mountains and plains. I shot arrows that penetrated the strongest of armor and defended castles where delicate damsels lived. The powerful, invincible, honorable, and courageous men captured my imagination, much more than the almost invisible women, who, if they were present at all, were usually portrayed as weak and fearful.

The girl who read Jules Verne and Walter Scott grew up to become the woman I am today. It was only recently that I thought to ask the question that should have been on my mind all along: Where were the stories about women, young girls, and teenage girls? How do we appear, other than garbed in beautiful dresses or topped with gorgeous hair? When do we come in and play a role beyond showing our skill at embroidery and serving others (by which I mean men) in everything?

I began to dig deeply inside the magical box of traditional folktales— Arabic, Russian, Indian, Scottish, and many others—and, as if I were Lewis Carroll's Alice, I discovered a parallel universe. I also read new stories, ones that had never been told to me, or to anyone I knew. We were never told stories about strong, courageous women who were smarter than the men were. We were never told stories about damsels who defended themselves without holding a weapon, who triumphed by dint of their intelligence and succeeded because they were wise.

Perhaps we were never told these stories because women have generally not been the ones responsible for reflecting upon their own history. We have always seen the world through masculine eyes: we, girls and women, have described the world and told our own stories through male eyes. The oral tradition, as anthologized by the Brothers Grimm, Alexander Afanasyev, Parker Fillmore, Andrew Lang, Francesc Maspons, and many others, mostly men, brought us the stories that have fueled our imaginations.

Folktales for Fearless Girls are the traditional stories I wish I could have read during my childhood: folktales in which heroic women are depicted as capable, courageous, and wise. These are stories that new readers like you will live in, just as I lived in the stories I read when I was young. Just as I did with those stories, these will have readers flying off to distant countries, galloping across mountains and plains, shooting arrows that penetrate the strongest of armor, and defending castles where defenseless men and women live. Courageous women who are powerful, honorable, and invincible will take their place right alongside men in readers' imaginations.

It is a gift to grow up with stories. The princes and princesses who fill our pages nourish our imaginations and spur our fantasies. But our gorgeous popular literary tradition reflects the society that once existed—it is filled with stories in which women are invisible, and because of that, it continues to teach us the same ideas. I believe that the best way to promote the values of freedom and equality is by creating a free and egalitarian collective imagination where both men and women play heroic roles. I hope you'll join me in enjoying these stories, and in recognizing the power and strength that woman all around the world possess.

Blancaflor

A Tale from Spain

any years ago, when the stars above had no names, a king and a queen ruled kindly and fairly in a distant kingdom. Though their lives were comfortable, they were unable to have a child, and this made them extremely unhappy.

As the years passed, the queen began to lose hope. Upset by what not having a child could mean for her husband and their kingdom, she decided to visit the devil. Though she hid her desperation as best she could, the devil, who was very cunning, sensed her misery immediately and knew he could take advantage of her.

"You will give birth to a son . . ." the devil said. After a pause, he added, "When he turns twenty, you must allow him to leave home."

The queen knew that by the time her son turned twenty, he would be a grown man and in control of his own life. She consented to the devil's demand, unable to see any other way out of her sad situation.

Soon after the queen's visit to the devil, she gave birth to the healthiest, best-looking, and strongest boy in all the kingdom. The royal family had so much wanted an heir that they spoiled him—and he didn't understand how lucky he was.

As the prince grew older, he became more impulsive and irresponsible. He grew to love gambling more than anything else in life. In fact, the prince became such a celebrated gambler that the devil realized the time had come to make good on the demand he had placed upon the queen. One night, he appeared before the prince disguised as a duke of a nearby kingdom and offered to play a game of cards. When the devil let the prince beat him, the prince, excited by the prospect of making an easy fortune, challenged the devil to play again the next day. It was in this second round that the devil revealed his true purpose: he won every game and left the prince without a penny to his name.

"I would keep playing you," the prince wept, "but I don't have any money left to gamble."

The devil gazed straight into his eyes, revealing his true identity, and whispered: "In that case, you can gamble your soul."

The prince accepted, desperate to win back all he had lost. But the devil won once more, and the prince was upset.

"To win back your soul, you must come to my castle," said the devil, who wasn't finished tormenting the prince yet. "I will give you three tasks. If you complete them, I will give you back your soul."

The prince realized he had no choice—without his soul, he would wither like a tree in the desert. Sad and downtrodden, he returned home to say good-bye to his parents. The king and queen remembered the promise the queen had made to the devil twenty years earlier, and, afraid of what would befall their son, they confessed the truth to him. The prince didn't fault his parents for the deal they had made, because he was certain he could easily complete the tasks the devil proposed and that his life would go back to normal.

And so the prince went in search of the devil's castle. He wandered back and forth throughout the countryside for a full day, not knowing quite how to reach it. Just as the sun was setting, he met an old woman, who asked him for something to eat. The prince gave her all that he had, and the grateful woman asked him if there was anything she could do for him in return.

"I'm on my way to the devil's castle," the prince answered. "I've been walking around all day, but I haven't been able to find it."

"You're near, but you won't get there unless you follow my instructions," the old woman said. "You must go to a stream near the River Hatred, where the devil's three daughters bathe. Once you get there, hide the clothes of Blancaflor, the youngest daughter. Don't return them until she promises to help you."

The prince walked on, across valleys, forests, and mountains until, through the clouds, he saw the rocky fortress that was the devil's castle. Along the side of the path he spotted a river, and found trees on its bank to hide behind as he waited for the devil's daughters to arrive. It was not long before they appeared and began to bathe in the river. After some time, the two older sisters came out and got dressed, immediately turning into doves and flying away. But the youngest daughter stayed in the water.

Blancaflor floated in the river pool, watching the clouds in the sky, hoping to reach them one day. "Anywhere but here," she murmured. The young woman did not want to get out of the water and get dressed, for she knew that the second she did, she would become a dove and have to fly back to the castle like her sisters.

She hated the boring routine her devil father imposed. He wouldn't let his daughters read, talk, or even think. Afraid to lose them, he had trapped the three women in the form of doves, imprisoning them in a castle that served as their cage.

Blancaflor felt hopeless. The only time she ever felt happy was when she was bathing in the river.

But when her skin began to wrinkle in the water, she knew it was time to get out. Droplets of water glistened on her skin. She walked over to the tree where she had left her clothes, but when she got there, she saw a young man she had never met holding her garments.

"I will give your clothes back if you promise to help me reach your father," the prince said.

Blancaflor lifted her head proudly; she was not going to let anyone scare her. Though the prince was asking her to help him, she saw an opportunity to help herself as well. Maybe this was her chance to escape, something she had dreamed about for so long.

If she accepted the prince's demand, she realized, she could have him help her outwit the beast defending the fortress, which awoke at any sound and would go back to sleep only if he heard the devil's voice. It was this beast that truly kept her trapped in the devil's castle.

"I set the terms here, not you," Blancaflor replied confidently. "I can assure you that you need me more than I need you. Follow me to my father's castle. And don't speak until I give you permission—but be sure to speak when I do."

Impressed by the young girl's poise, the prince accepted at once—his only desire was to win back his soul. He returned her clothes and, once she was dressed, Blancaflor turned into a dove as she always had. Together, the two went back to the castle.

The devil wasn't surprised to see the prince. Ready to trick him once again, he revealed the three challenges.

"Your first task is to flatten and plow that hill. Then plant wheat; when it's grown, harvest it, grind the grain, and bring me a loaf of bread tomorrow."

Upon understanding that the devil had set him an impossible task, the prince's heart sank. He realized that instead of returning to his parents, he would spend the rest of his days withering away in the devil's castle.

Blancaflor heard him weeping. She knew what her father was like, but this time, she was not going to let him succeed. She was determined to escape the prison in which she lived, and to help the prince escape as well.

"I promised to help you," she said. "And I am as good as my word."

That night, she plowed the earth on the nearby hill with her magical wings and planted the field. Her claws harvested the wheat and her feathers ground the wheat into flour. When the prince awoke, he saw a warm loaf of bread before him, which he took to the devil.

"You wouldn't have been able to plow a single foot of that field without Blancaflor's help," the devil bellowed. He tossed the bread into the fire. "Your second task is to turn this field into a vineyard and bring me a bottle of wine in the afternoon."

The prince knew that the devil had set another impossible task, so he asked Blancaflor for help once again. She fluttered around him and promised to bring him a bottle of wine. Then she added, "Remember to speak when I ask you to. If you refuse, you will have failed to keep up your part of the bargain."

The young man looked into her eyes and nodded. So off Blancaflor flew, until she saw the field, which had become dry and barren. She begged the clouds for water and the sun to change hours into days. She asked the wind to blow the leaves off the grapevines. Then, with her magical wings, she harvested the field. Her claws trampled the grapes and her wings fermented the wine. Then she handed the bottle over to the prince, who brought it to the devil.

The devil knew that Blancaflor had helped the prince yet again. Without her, how could he have performed such tasks? The third chore, though, would be extremely difficult, even for her.

"I would like to give my youngest daughter the ring at the bottom of the sea. Bring it to me."

Once again, the prince asked Blancaflor for help, for he was incapable of doing what the devil had requested. This time, however, Blancaflor wept in sorrow, for she knew her father had asked for the Ring of Forgetfulness. If she were to place this ring on a finger on her right hand, everyone she knew except her father would forget her.

She could imagine no worse punishment.

The prince tried to reassure her.

Tears fell from Blancaflor's eyes, but she flew off to find the ring. She knew that if she didn't help the prince, he would remain locked up in the castle, and she along with him. She had to try.

Blancaflor flew to the sea and dove down to the very bottom. When she found the ring, she devised a plan: she pulled off the longest feather in her right wing.

When she returned to her father's castle, Blancaflor gave the ring to the prince, who presented it to the devil. But when he allowed his daughter to resume her human form and he tried to put the ring on her, he realized that she was missing her right ring finger—just where she had pulled out the feather.

The devil growled. "You will wear the ring on your left hand instead," he decreed. "He who loves you will forget you the moment anyone but you embraces him."

Blancaflor's heart sank, but she was glad to know that her plan had been partially successful: the prince was free. All that remained was for him to fulfill the last part of his promise and help her obtain her own freedom as well.

As it grew dark, Blancaflor set out to escape from the castle with the prince. As they ran through the corridors, the dreaded beast heard their footsteps and lifted his head up to sniff the night air.

"The time has come for you to speak up," whispered Blancaflor. "Don't be afraid. All you have to say is this: 'The free person is the one who dreams, not the one who flies.'"

The prince immediately understood the significance of those words.

They sounded like something the devil himself would say; they were a whisper that would silence the beast, tricking him into thinking that the devil was speaking. By speaking these words, he could keep the devil asleep and help Blancaflor gain her freedom.

The prince gathered his courage and slowly said the words. The beast dropped his head and went back to sleep, and the prince and Blancaflor ran for the stable, where two horses—named Swift Wind and Deep Thought—awaited them.

While Blancaflor kept a lookout, she asked the prince to saddle Deep Thought.

"And grab that old rusted sword you see on the ground," she said to the prince. "If you don't, my father will capture us."

The prince went into the stable and saw a young, powerful stallion. It was Swift Wind. Deep Thought, an old and skinny coatrack of a horse, was beside him. The prince saw the rusty sword on the ground and, lying next to it, a shiny new sword. Sure that Blancaflor had made a mistake, he saddled Swift Wind and took the shiny sword. Blancaflor saw what he had done, but the urgency of their escape weighed heavily on her, and she got on Swift Wind without another word.

They galloped through the dark night toward the spot where the sun rose. As soon as they saw daylight, they would be free of the devil.

But the devil, who was aware of their escape even without the help of his beast, saddled Deep Thought and galloped through the night, following closely on their tail. When he approached them, he and his horse became an enormous animal, one that was faster, more powerful, and even crueler than the devil himself.

"Don't look back," the prince said to Blancaflor as soon as he saw her father coming after them. "Don't be afraid. We're riding the fastest horse in the world."

"You're mistaken," Blancaflor replied. "Only on Deep Thought's back could we have escaped. Now we need to face the monster that my father has become."

Blancaflor reached into her pocket and pulled out a handful of seeds, which she dropped behind the horse's flank. As they fell, they turned into balls of fire, and the devil reared back until he was able to put them out. Then Blancaflor asked the prince for the rusted sword. When he produced the shiny sword instead, she knew that it would prove useless in battle, as it did not possess the power hidden inside the rusty old blade. Thinking quickly, Blancaflor turned into a bird and stretched her wings until they became the size of an eagle's. She gripped the shiny sword in her powerful claws and pinned her father to the ground with so much strength that the earth beneath him split in two, creating a gulf so deep that he could not get out.

And so she and the prince were able to escape from the devil and his castle.

Once they were alone, Blancaflor regained her human form. Yet she was deeply troubled. She knew that her father's final curse had taken hold when he put the ring on her left finger, and that she would be forgotten the second anyone else hugged the prince. This upset her greatly, for over the course of their trials and adventures together, the two had fallen in love.

The prince returned to his kingdom with Blancaflor at his side. He forbade anyone to hug him, so that he would never forget his one true love. Her embraces were the only ones he permitted.

One day, the prince and Blancaflor visited a far-off country. Unaware of the curse, the king of that country hugged the prince in welcome, then presented his daughter to the prince and offered her hand in marriage. The prince, upon whom the curse had taken its toll the moment the king had hugged him, had already forgotten Blancaflor entirely, and he agreed to marry the king's daughter. But the princess was in fact the devil in disguise—he had managed to escape from the pit Blancaflor had left him in.

When the wedding day arrived, Blancaflor returned to the kingdom dressed as a craftsperson.

"Your Majesties," she said to the prince and princess, "I come from far away to bring you the most precious thing I have." She produced a magical stone and a cage.

What strange gifts, thought the prince. But aloud he said, "Thank you for your generosity."

Later, after the prince was asleep, the devil took off his human form and, under the glow of the moonlight, wished to know why his daughter had offered such odd gifts. As soon as he voiced his question, the stone began to speak.

"I am the stone of sorrow, what your daughter feels in her heart, ever since she worked her magic to help free the prince but was never truly freed herself. She grew the wheat and made the bread that the prince brought to you. And she harvested the grapes to make the wine that he brought to you as well. And she retrieved the ring from the bottom of the sea. All in the hopes of freedom."

The voice of the stone awoke the prince, who, little by little, began to remember.

The devil then asked the cage why his daughter had brought it as a gift.

"I've come so that Blancaflor can live inside my bars," the cage answered. "She suffers greatly from being forgotten—so greatly that she prefers to live like a caged dove."

At that very moment, with the voice of the cage echoing through the room, the curse was lifted. The prince remembered everything and ran to Blancaflor. When he found her, he took the Ring of Forgetfulness, now useless with the spell broken, off her left hand. He threw it back into the sea, from which he now realized it never should have been taken.

Blancaflor, the only person to have ever tricked the devil and escaped from his grasp, became the wisest and most just queen who ever lived. And from that moment on, not a single person forgot her ever again.

Kupti and Imani

A Tale from India

In a far-off country lived a king with his two daughters, Kupti and Imani. The king loved his daughters more than anything in the world, and he especially loved talking with them during long summer afternoons. He planned to give both of them a beautiful future in which they could marry for love and not money.

One day, while the sun was going down, he addressed Kupti, his eldest daughter: "Dearest daughter, are you happy with the idea of inheriting my wealth?"

Kupti did not understand why her father asked her something so obvious. Of course she was happy to inherit her father's fortune! She could not imagine anyone who deserved riches more than she.

The next day, as the sun was setting, the king spoke to Imani, his younger daughter. He asked her the same question he had asked her older sister. Imani replied, "Father, I am grateful to you for your generosity, but I would like to give up my inheritance. I would prefer to seek my own fortune."

The king was surprised to hear her answer. He could not understand why she felt this way, but he decided to let her do as she pleased. With great sadness in his heart, he told her that if she wanted to seek her own fortune, she would have to leave the palace. Only by shedding the privileges of a princess would she be able to test her own abilities.

Imani understood her father's demand, and so she left the palace, searching for her path forward. She went to see a wise old man, known as a fakir, who was renowned the world over for his simplicity. He was so poor and lived in such misery that he hardly had a thing to eat. Worse, one of his legs hurt so much that he limped. Imani thought she could be of great help to him, so she asked him for shelter.

The old man could not understand why a princess would want to live with him. He glanced around, looking for some indication that he was merely dreaming. But, acknowledging that he was awake, all he could do was confirm that the princess was indeed there, in the flesh, and so he agreed to give her shelter.

When they reached the shack where he lived, the fakir sadly inspected his rickety straw bed. Could a princess actually sleep in it? Then he glanced at his cooking pot and clay jar of water, the only implements in his kitchen: What kind of dinner could he make her with the few root vegetables he had? He was only a poor fakir, a man resigned to poverty, something he could not change.

Imani smiled as she saw the inside of his shack. His home was neat and clean, warmed by a ray of light. She was grateful for the hut's simplicity, so different from the palace riches she was used to. She remembered her father, the king, who had told her that she had the ability to shape her own life. She considered how to go about it.

"Do you have any money?" she asked the fakir, the beginnings of a plan taking shape in her mind.

"I think I have a copper coin somewhere around here," he answered tentatively.

The princess helped him find the coin, which was worth less than a penny. She found it half-buried in the dirt floor. Then she asked him to borrow a loom and a spinning wheel from a neighbor.

The old fakir walked slowly down the street, and by the end of the morning, he had obtained what the princess had asked for.

Meanwhile, Imani had gone to the market and bought some rosemary oil and a pound of flax. When she returned to the shack, she asked the old man to lie down, and she rubbed the rosemary oil on his bad leg for an hour. Then she told him to rest. The fakir fell asleep listening to the soft spinning of the borrowed wheel. He awoke the next morning to the same sound; Imani had spent the entire night at the loom, making the finest thread the fakir had ever seen in his life.

Although she was very tired, the princess sat all day at the loom. Just as the sun was about to set, she finished weaving a beautiful cloth that, in the moonlight, seemed to be made of silver threads.

"Go to the market and sell my cloth," she said to the fakir. "While you do that, I shall rest."

The old man admired the beautiful cloth without understanding where something that beautiful had come from. How much could he ask for it? Never in his life had he felt anything so precious.

"Ask for two pieces of gold," said Imani, as if she had read his thoughts.

Soon the fakir was showing the cloth to people in the market. He limped from stand to stand, holding out the cloth for all to see.

That night, Princess Kupti went to the market and saw the fabric's brilliant silver sparkles. She went over to the fakir to buy it.

"You can have it for two pieces of gold," he told her.

The princess happily paid the price, gave the cloth to her servant, and returned to the palace. When the fakir returned home with the gold coins, he gave them to Imani, who used them to buy a spinning wheel and loom of her own. She sent the fakir to return the borrowed ones and, as a sign of her gratitude, gave the owners a ball of her very best yarn.

Each morning, Imani would get up with the sun and go to the market with a copper coin. She would buy a small bottle of rosemary oil and a pound of flax, then return to the shack and rub the fakir's injured leg for one hour with the oil. Then she would spin the finest of threads from the flax. She used the thread to make the most beautiful fabric, which the fakir would sell at the market for two pieces of gold. After each sale, she would set aside a copper coin and enough money to buy some food. The rest of the money she hid in a hole they dug in the shack.

Imani did this day after day, week after week, not caring that months and seasons passed. Her textiles became finer and more delicate as time went by, and they became celebrated throughout the city. The fakir, who barely limped now after Imani's treatment, would go to the market each day and sell whatever the princess made.

After some time, Imani realized that they would have to leave the shack:

her fabric had sold so successfully that there was no space left in their small home to store all the gold coins she had accumulated. She hired an architect and builders to construct a new house for her and the fakir. When it was done, it was simple, elegant, and so beautiful that even the king heard about it. When he found out that his daughter owned it, he smiled in satisfaction.

Kupti, however, felt pangs of jealousy. Since her sister had left the palace, the weight of being heir to the king's fortune had fallen entirely on her shoulders, and the thought of her future responsibilities weighed her down. She was dismayed by the idea of having to rule the kingdom one day, and preferred to simply laze about and surround herself with fancy things. She wished for her sister to return to the palace and share the burden with her.

But the king remained happy. "My younger daughter, Imani, said she wanted to amass her own wealth," the king stated proudly. "And she is doing it." He was glad to know that Imani was doing well, especially before leaving on his journey to the neighboring kingdom of Dûr, as he would be gone for a long period of time.

Before he left, he asked both of his daughters what they wanted as gifts. Kupti requested a ruby necklace, for she couldn't think of anything that would make for a more expensive gift.

Imani, on the contrary, asked for nothing.

She must need something, the king thought. He sent a messenger to her house. "Tell me what she needs and I will bring it back with me," he ordered.

When the messenger reached Imani's home, he found her busy at work. She was trying to untangle a skein of thread without tearing it. She was so absorbed in her task that she didn't even notice the messenger. "Patience," she said to herself, trying not to get frustrated. "I need patience. . . ."

The royal messenger returned to the palace and told the king that Princess Imani needed patience. "And she must have great need of it, for she repeated it many times," he added.

"Is that so?" replied the king, somewhat surprised. "I hope that they sell patience in Dûr. I've never seen patience, but if they sell it, I will buy it all up."

The king set off on his journey. When he had completed his work in Dûr, he bought the most expensive ruby necklace he could find for Kupti. "Go to the market and buy me patience," he then ordered his servant. "If it's not for sale, ask the people there where it can be bought. Don't come back without it."

The servant thought that patience would be impossible to buy, but he went to the marketplace regardless, for his king had made his request. "I want to buy patience! Patience! I need to buy patience!" he shouted in the middle of the market crowd.

It didn't take long for Sabar Khan, the young and handsome king of Dûr, to hear that someone wanted to buy patience. He was a curious king with a good sense of humor—he so much wanted to meet this peculiar buyer. When the servant met the king, he explained that he needed patience for Imani, his own king's daughter.

In the language of the kingdom of Dûr, Sabar—this king's first name— meant "patience," so King Sabar decided to play a trick on the servant.

"I can imagine how much patience the princess must have if she wants to buy some more. Tell her that there is patience in my kingdom, but it can't be bought or sold."

The servant didn't want to give up. He told King Sabar that Princess Imani was intelligent, determined, and hardworking, and that she had a large and generous heart.

"That's wonderful," King Sabar said. "Let me give you something." And Sabar Khan gave the servant a jewelry box with a fan inside. He closed it carefully, ordering the messenger to deliver it to the princess.

"This box doesn't have a lock or key. But don't worry about the safety of what's inside; it will only open when the person who needs what's inside touches it." Then he added: "When she opens it, she will find patience, though I'm not sure it will be the kind of patience she is looking for."

When the servant returned with the jewelry box, his king was ready to leave Dûr and return to his kingdom. After a long journey back, he reached the palace, where he distributed his gifts. Kupti put on the necklace with a yawn and promptly went along her way. Imani thanked her father for the jewelry box and went back home with it, though she did not know what it contained.

When Imani returned, the fakir did all he could to open the box, but to no avail. He simply couldn't get it to open. Then Imani tried it. Just as her hands touched the top, the box miraculously opened! Imani looked inside and saw a beautiful object, which she picked up. When she saw that it was a fan, she opened it up and began to fan herself.

She waved the fan once, twice, three times—and all of a sudden, Sabar Khan appeared. "You have summoned me by fanning yourself three times," the king explained. "I can give you what you've asked for. If you want me to go away, you have to do one of two things: close the fan or tap it on the table. I will go back to my palace just as I arrived here, one, two, three."

"But I haven't summoned anyone. And I haven't asked for anything," Imani replied.

"You asked for patience," the king said. "And since that's my name, here I am, at your service."

At that, the fakir thought it polite to welcome Sabar Khan into their home. Feeling more at ease, the king began to tell Imani and the fakir about his life, and when he discovered that he shared a love of chess with the fakir, they began a game and taught Imani to play as well.

They so enjoyed one another's company that Sabar Khan began to visit the fakir and Imani's house almost every day. At times they played games of chess late into the night, sometimes so late that the king spent the night at their house. The fakir and Imani even designated a room for the king to use whenever he slept over, so that he could spend the night there and rest and return to his kingdom in the morning.

Soon, the people of the kingdom began to gossip about a rich and handsome young man living in Imani's house. Kupti overheard this gossip and was determined to find out the truth. She knew the time had come to visit her sister, a thing she hadn't done since Imani had left the palace all those months ago. Though she would never say it aloud, she was jealous of her

sister, who she saw had set up her life in a way that gave her the freedom to do as she pleased.

Full of bitterness, Kupti went to her sister's house. Though she made polite conversation with both Imani and the fakir throughout the day, Kupti enacted her true plan at one quiet point that afternoon when she furtively entered Sabar Khan's bedroom and sprinkled a powerful poisonous dust between the sheets.

As soon as Kupti left, Imani fanned herself three times: she wanted to talk to the king of Dûr about her sister's visit. They discussed Kupti's strange behavior at length, after which the king and the fakir turned to a game of chess. And because the hour got so late, Sabar Khan made the decision to spend the night at his friends' home.

As he slept in his poison-filled bed, the dust seeped into his skin.

When the young king returned to Dûr in the morning, he felt sick. His advisers called doctors and wise men from across the kingdom, but none could determine the cause of the king's ailments. He grew worse by the day; his fever increased and the pain became more and more pronounced. His subjects grew fearful that he might die.

Far from Dûr, Princess Imani and the fakir became worried. They had called their friend repeatedly with the fan, but he wasn't appearing. Their concern grew so great that Imani knew she had to act.

"I am going to Dûr to see what's going on," the princess said to the fakir. "Maybe he needs our help."

Imani set out on her journey dressed in the rags of a fakir so that no one would recognize her. She walked for two days straight without resting, and by the second night, she was so exhausted that she decided to lie down under a tree branch for a quick rest. Though she was very tired, she could not fall asleep—her mind raced with concern for Sabar Khan.

As she lay there, she heard two monkeys in the branches above her head talking to each other. "The king of Dûr is dying," the first monkey said. "Kupti, a princess from a neighboring kingdom, spread poisonous dust between his bedsheets."

"Are you sure?" the second monkey asked.

"The birds have told me," the first monkey replied. "They know all, since they are everywhere and see everything."

"How sad," the second monkey answered. "The king of Dûr is a good ruler. Boiling the berries of this tree in hot water could cure him. He would recover in three days."

Imani heard the monkeys' whole conversation. She wasn't sure whether it had been real or just a dream born of her exhaustion, but she gathered all the berries she could just in case and went on her way to Dûr without another stop.

When she arrived, though, she realized that she wasn't sure where the king's palace was, or whether she'd be allowed in. In all the time she had known Sabar Khan, he had always come to her home, and no one in the kingdom of Dûr knew who she was. So she went straight to the market and walked down its alleys, thinking that this would be her best chance of reaching the king.

"Medicine for sale!" she shouted, still dressed in her outfit of rags. "Is there anyone in need of medicine to cure fevers and poisonings?"

A man who thought she was a young fakir came over to the princess and said: "Come with me to the palace. Our king is in fact very sick. Perhaps your medicine will help him."

The man brought Imani to the palace, but even though she stated that she had a cure for the king, the guards stopped her. All of the other healers had been wealthy doctors and renowned wise men, and they were reluctant to let a poor fakir touch their noble ruler. Still she refused to give up. She was so persistent in her attempts to see the king that, finally, the guards relented.

She entered the king's chambers, stating, "I need only a room and a pot to boil water."

The king's advisers were surprised that she asked for so little; the doctors and wise men had all asked for expensive herbs, rare minerals, and other extravagant items.

They gave her what she asked for. When the water boiled, she threw the berries into the pot and asked the king's servants to bathe him in the water. They did as she commanded, and later that day, for the first time since he had fallen ill, the king slept peacefully.

The following day, Imani once again boiled water and threw berries in it. She asked the servants to wet the king's lips with the potion. They did as she commanded, and soon thereafter, the king was hungry and thirsty, his appetite returned to him. On the third day, Imani ordered the servants to wrap the king's feet in the berry water. The servants obeyed, and very soon thereafter, the king stood up and was able to walk. Though he was still weak, he was clearly on his way to a full recovery.

The next day, Imani saw that Sabar Khan was doing well, and she knew the time had come to leave. Before she departed, the king insisted on meeting the illustrious doctor who had saved his life. Though his advisers told him that the doctor was just a young fakir, the king nevertheless wanted to show his gratitude.

When Imani met the king wearing her fakir rags, Sabar Khan tried to give her huge sums of money to show his appreciation. But Imani did not desire riches.

"I insist," said the king. "I would be deeply offended if the person who saved my life refused to accept my gift."

"In that case," replied Imani deeply, pretending to be a man, "I would be pleased to have the signet ring on your finger and one of your handkerchiefs."

"I have objects that are worth much more," the king told her, "but if that is all you want, you shall have them."

The king took a handkerchief from inside his cape and pulled the ring off his finger, and handed both objects to Imani. She left at once, without the king recognizing her for who she truly was.

After some time, the king recovered completely. By then, both his life and the lives of Imani and the fakir had gone back to normal. One day, Imani, who missed her visits with Sabar Khan, used the fan to call him to her. The young king appeared immediately, and as so much time had passed since they had last met, they spent the entire evening and long into the night engaged in lively conversation. Just as the sun was about to rise, the king told them about the young fakir who had cured him. He spoke of how grateful he was to his mysterious healer, and how sad he was to have only been able to give him his signet ring and a handkerchief.

Imani smiled and took out the ring and the handkerchief from her pocket.

"Is this what your healer requested from you?" she asked, smiling broadly.

Sabar Khan looked into Imani's eyes and knew at once that she had been the young fakir.

"I don't believe the berries made me better," the king answered. "It was being close to you, Imani."

Indeed, Sabar Khan had been in love with Imani from the very first day he had met her, from the very first time she had used the fan to summon him. Right then and there, he asked her to be the queen of his kingdom. He would not return without her, he declared.

The princess, who had herself also fallen in love the very first day she had met Sabar Khan, happily agreed, and went to her father's palace to tell him of her plans.

"I know that there is no man on earth who is happier than your future husband," the king responded when Imani told him her news. "Just as I know that there is no man on this earth prouder of his daughter than I am."

Standing nearby, Kupti overheard her father's words. She approached her sister, knowing that she had been wrong to ever try to interfere. "Please forgive me, dearest sister," she implored. "I acted out of spite, for I was jealous of your courage. But from you I have learned that I, too, can act with bravery and be the one who determines my own future. From this moment on, I will act in just such a way."

Imani embraced her sister, whom she knew to be sincere in her apology. And so it was that Imani's determination and initiative led not only to her own happiness, but to that of her sister as well.

A Wise Girl

A Tale from Russia

asha, the daughter of a poor shepherd, lived with her father in a remote cottage. A bright girl, she dreamed of traveling the world one day, when she had the money to afford it.

Some afternoons, Masha would go to the village square, and she would often hear the neighbors grumbling. Many of them complained about the richest farmer in the village, a greedy man with no scruples.

One night, upon returning home, Masha found her father staring sadly at the floor.

"What's wrong, Father?" she asked.

"I've worked all week for the rich farmer," the shepherd answered. "He promised to give me a calf as payment, but now he's changed his mind and is refusing to keep his word."

"The farmer is not a trustworthy man," Masha replied. "You should go and see the mayor. He will make the farmer keep his promise."

The next day, the shepherd went to pay a visit to the mayor. Though he listened very carefully, the mayor was a young man with little experience, and he didn't know what to do.

He decided to call the farmer to hear his side of the story, and when the farmer gave excuse after excuse, the mayor still wasn't sure whom to trust.

So he came up with a plan: he would pose a riddle to both the farmer and the shepherd, and when he saw how each of them solved it, he would know what kind of person each of them was.

"Whoever answers best will get the calf," he said.

"Here is my riddle: Tell me, what is the fastest thing in the world, the sweetest thing in the world, and the richest thing in the world? Give me your answers by this time tomorrow."

The farmer returned happily to his home, sure that he knew the answer to the riddle. The shepherd, on the other hand, went back to his cottage more troubled than when he had left—the more he thought about the riddle, the less sure he was about the right answer.

The moment he saw his wife, the greedy farmer explained the situation. "The answer is oh so easy," he crowed. "In fact, I think he is doing me a favor. The answer is just under my nose."

The farmer's wife had always admired her husband, who she thought was very intelligent. She sat down and listened attentively as he explained his answer.

"You'll see," the farmer said. "The fastest thing on earth is our gray mare. Whenever we go to the fields, the mare is already there. The sweetest thing in the world is, of course, our honey. Do you remember when I gave the mayor a jar of our best honey? Surely he posed that question remembering our gift."

He went on: "As for the richest, no one in this village has accumulated as much wealth as I have, so the answer is surely our chest filled with gold coins."

The farmer was so sure he had cracked the riddle that he and his wife celebrated by having a most delicious dinner. They saw themselves selling the calf for a nice sum, which would make them all the richer.

Meanwhile, at the shepherd's house, Masha comforted her father. He couldn't come up with an answer to the mayor's riddle and seemed so defeated by misfortune, so weighed down by his troubles, that he was unable to kill a fly, let alone protest any injustice. Masha knew she had to cheer him up, and that there was only one way to do so: by figuring out the answer to the riddle that was giving him such a headache.

"Father," she started, "there's nothing faster than our minds. One second our thoughts are here, next second they are at a river. Nothing moves faster than our thoughts! As for the sweetest thing in the world: think about the sleep that comes over you the moment you lie down in your bed. Can you imagine anything sweeter than that? As for richness: the richest thing in the world is that which gives us all that we need. Therefore, isn't the earth the richest thing in the world?"

The shepherd raised his eyes from the floor and looked at his daughter. This time she had revealed not only the brilliance of her mind, but also her great sensitivity—only with those two traits could anyone solve such a complicated riddle so well.

The following day the farmer came to the mayor's chambers with a bag of pears, which he had on hand to give to the mayor once he was told that he could keep the calf. The shepherd, on the other hand, came empty-handed, though he was less gloomy than he had been the day before.

The mayor received them immediately, wanting to put an end to their dispute.

"So," he said, "do you know what is the fastest thing in the world, the sweetest thing in the world, and the richest thing in the world?"

The farmer hurried to reply, not waiting for the mayor to give him permission to speak. "The fastest thing in the world is my gray mare, since no other animal can gallop ahead of her," he answered, repeating the words he had spoken to his wife. "The sweetest thing, as you know, is the honey from my beehive. And, of course, the richest thing is my chest filled with gold coins."

The mayor did all he could to hide his surprise, for the answer the farmer had given was one that only a stubborn, self-centered, and narrow-minded person would give. He said nothing, and then glanced at the shepherd and asked him to respond.

"Dear sir," began the shepherd, "I have neither the intelligence nor the clarity to answer your question correctly. I am, however, blessed to be the father of an intelligent and generous daughter who has given me the following answer.

"The fastest thing is our minds—with them we can travel across the world faster than a rooster's crow. The sweetest thing is the sleep that comes over us after a very tiring day. And the richest thing is the generous earth that gives us the food and sustenance we need in order to live."

The mayor applauded the shepherd for his answer, which he knew to be wise, and declared that the shepherd was the rightful owner of the calf. And he said nothing to the farmer, who left in such a huff that he forgot his sack of pears.

Curious about the daughter whom the good shepherd had so generously praised, the mayor gave him ten eggs to give to her.

"Ask your daughter to bring me a chicken from each egg tomorrow," he commanded.

The shepherd glanced at the mayor in disbelief. Had he heard correctly? That was impossible. But he didn't dare say a single word and instead returned home heavyhearted. Though he had won the competition over the riddle, he had also put his daughter in a terrible position.

When Masha saw the eggs and heard her father explain the mayor's wishes, she began to laugh. Without saying anything about the ten chickens, she made a large omelet and shared it with all their neighbors. The poor shepherd trusted in his daughter, but he feared that this time, she would be unable to meet the challenge.

The next day, Masha awoke feeling as if she were at the start of a journey, like a person beginning a wonderful new book, or someone gazing up at the stars, trying to match them to a map of the heavens. She had a plan in mind, and she was curious to find out how the young mayor would respond to the challenge she would ask her father to bring to him.

"Take a handful of millet to the mayor," Masha said to her father. "Tell him to plant it, cultivate it, and harvest it tomorrow; I'll bring the ten chicks then, so that they can eat his ripe grain."

The poor shepherd glanced first at the handful of millet, then at his daughter. He saw a glow in her eyes, and he understood how confident she was in her words and deeds. Though he didn't understand what all this carrying of millet and eggs back and forth meant, he didn't hesitate to relay Masha's orders. When the mayor heard her challenge, he belted out a big laugh. He told the shepherd that he wanted to meet her.

"But tell her not to come during the day or the night, not on horseback or by foot, not dressed or naked," he added.

Masha was happy with the young mayor's answer. She realized that she wanted to meet him as well, since he seemed very bright and had a good sense of humor. The young woman waited until the morning, at which point she took off her clothes and wrapped herself up in a red fisherman's net. Then she tied a board to a goat's harness, climbed atop the board, and rode that way to the mayor.

When the mayor saw her, he could do nothing but praise the young woman's imagination.

"Here I am," she said to him. "I haven't come during the day or night, since it is now morning, and in between the two. I am not on horseback or on foot, since I am being dragged behind a goat. And I am also not dressed, since a net really isn't a garment, nor am I naked, since you cannot see my body."

The young mayor was so charmed by Masha's cleverness that he asked her to marry him and live in his chambers. Having heard that Masha loved to read, he added, "There's a library here that you can visit anytime."

Masha considered his offer. "I accept on the condition that you will never

interfere in my freedom and that I can do whatever I want and go wherever I please. If you stop me, I will go back to my cottage."

The young mayor agreed, and noted that he also had one condition. "You must never interfere in my affairs. If you do, you will have to go back to your cottage as well."

Masha thought that seemed fair, so the couple got married and were very happy; not only did they have love and good fortune, they also respected each other.

One day, Masha went out for a walk and came across a man crying bitterly. "Can I be of help?" the young woman asked.

The man explained that his mare had just given birth to a foal, but his neighbor had stolen it.

"How was he able to do that?" Masha asked.

"The foal walked to my neighbor's wagon and fell asleep under it, and now my neighbor says that his wagon birthed the foal and it is his!"

"That's not right!" Masha protested. "Go and tell the mayor. He is a just man. Let him decide who is entitled to the foal."

She was very surprised when the man said that he had already seen the mayor, who had ruled that the man who found the foal under his wagon was the true owner.

Masha decided that her husband must not have understood this man's story, because his decision was so clearly wrong. She thought it was only right to intervene.

"Come back to see the mayor this afternoon. Bring a fishnet and stretch it along the road," Masha told the man. "When the mayor sees you, he will ask what you are doing. In response, you must repeat what I tell you word for word. He will then realize his mistake and correct it." And she told him the words to say to the mayor on the road.

The man was very grateful to Masha. He promised not to reveal that she had come up with this clever plan.

A few hours later, as the sun was going down, the mayor went out for a walk. Before long, he found the man, who had followed Masha's instructions and stretched a fishnet across the road. The mayor, confused, asked him what he was doing.

Still following what Masha had said, the man explained that he was fishing. At that, the mayor answered: "There's no way to catch fish on a dusty road."

The mayor said exactly what the man had hoped to hear. "Well," he replied, repeating Masha's words, "it's just as easy for me to catch fish on a dusty road as it is for a wagon to give birth to a foal."

The mayor immediately realized that he had ruled incorrectly earlier that day. Yet he sensed that someone else had come up with this answer, and he asked the man where he had gotten that idea. The man, in his happiness at the mayor's changed ruling, forgot his promise to Masha and told him the truth.

The mayor felt betrayed. He went back home and sought out Masha in his chambers.

"I could have asked for many things, but I asked only that you not

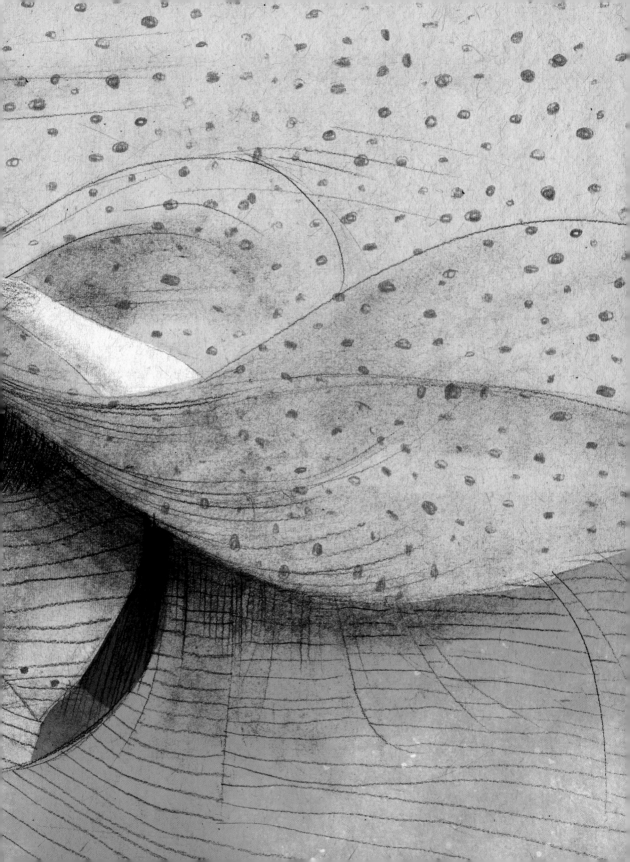

interfere," he sadly said to his wife. "You have betrayed me, so you must leave my house and go back to your cottage, as we had agreed."

Masha realized she had broken her promise. Instead of begging her husband to reconsider and forgive her, she decided to speak honestly and from her heart. She reminded him how happy they had been together and she asked him if they could continue to be friends once she left. The mayor liked this plan, and so, to remember their past, they had one final delicious dinner in which both laughed and rejoiced.

"Dear husband," Masha suddenly said, "I will be leaving soon, but I would like to take something with me as a remembrance of what I most like and appreciate about this house. Would that be all right?"

Her husband nodded with his eyes half-closed, since the lavish dinner had tired him. As he fell into a deep sleep, Masha put her plan in motion. She took out several yards of cloth from a chest and wrapped her husband up, then dragged him to their wagon and put him inside.

The following day, when the sun was directly overhead, the mayor woke up with a start, still in the wagon. Through the door of the cottage, he saw Masha busily going about her day.

"What's going on?" he asked her, disconcerted.

She smiled as she drew the curtains in her cottage.

"Nothing, dear husband. I have simply done what you allowed me. I have returned to my father's cottage and brought with me what I most like and appreciate from what had been my house."

The young mayor looked at himself and smiled. He understood how clever Masha had been, once again. He realized that asking her not to inter-fere in his affairs was like asking a bird not to fly.

"I know that you are not only intelligent, but also generous," he said to her. "I will forgive you if you accept my new proposal."

Masha, thinking that he would ask her to return home, prepared to say yes. Instead, her husband asked for her help in all his affairs, since she was better prepared than he was and, without a doubt, she was the smartest person he had ever met. She agreed, and together they settled affairs of state wisely for many years.

Lady Ragnell

A Tale from England

In a famous kingdom known as Camelot, there was a just king known for his courage, who relied on twelve knights to maintain peace in the region. They were known as King Arthur and the Knights of the Round Table.

While riding his horse in the Inglewood Forest one afternoon, King Arthur glimpsed a beautiful stag through the mist. Not wanting to scare him off, the king separated from the rest of his huntsmen so that he could approach the stag alone. Little did he realize that he was in fact falling into a trap set by Sir Gromer Somer Joure, a ruthless sorcerer who terrorized anyone who crossed his path.

Before King Arthur saw the sorcerer, the king's faithful horse, Hengroen, sensed his powerful presence and warned his master by neighing and scraping his hooves on the ground. The king took the warning to heart, but he wasn't afraid of anything; he placed his right hand on his sword and dug his spurs into his steed to continue stalking the stag.

Suddenly, Sir Gromer shot out from the fog, dressed head to toe in daunting black armor. He stood in the king's path, preparing to attack, but before he did so, he said, "I will spare your life if you return here in a year and answer the following question."

Though King Arthur wasn't afraid to fight, he understood that against Sir Gromer's magical powers, he was at a disadvantage. The king lowered his sword, thinking that a year was more than enough time to find the answer to any question, no matter how difficult. He could consult wise men in other kingdoms and bring together scholars and experts, if necessary.

"And if I give you the wrong answer?" the king wanted to know.

"Then I will put you to death," declared Sir Gromer Somer Joure.

Sir Arthur felt a chill go down his spine, but he wouldn't back down now. "Ask your question," he said resolutely.

The Knight of the Black Armor faced him squarely and asked: "What is it that women most desire?" After asking this question, Sir Gromer vanished into a dark cloud of smoke.

King Arthur spurred his horse, and Hengroen galloped away as fast as he could. When he reached his castle, the king locked himself away as he tried to find the right answer. But all he could think of was the evil look on Sir Gromer's face as he threatened to kill him in a year's time.

Sir Gawain, King Arthur's nephew, realized that something was preoccupying the king. He loved and admired his uncle, and so, despite the king's wish to hide his concern, Gawain asked what was bothering him. The king shared his torment and felt better immediately, hopeful that his nephew would know the answer to Sir Gromer's question. For although Sir Gawain wasn't betrothed, he was the favorite of the ladies of the court, and King Arthur felt sure that he would be able to respond wisely.

After hearing the king's question, the young knight proposed something quite unusual: that he and the king travel through the kingdom and ask the women they encountered what they desired most.

"We won't travel together," his nephew added, "but each of us will write down the answers we receive in a ledger. At the end of our journey, we will meet up, compare the answers, and know what to say to Sir Gromer."

So the following morning, they each set off on their long journeys, going in separate directions. They asked the women they met along the way what they desired most.

"I want to marry the man of my choice," one responded.

"I want to go to war with my husband," another confessed.

"I would like to travel to far-off places," added still another.

A few days before the year had passed, King Arthur and Sir Gawain met up once again at the castle. The responses they had gathered were all so different that they couldn't figure out which would be the correct answer.

So King Arthur once again went on horseback to Inglewood Forest looking for the Knight of the Black Armor, hoping to change their agreement before the year was out.

Instead of finding Sir Gromer, though, he found a woman in the forest running from tree to tree as if trying to hide from someone. The king approached her to offer his help, but before he could say anything, the woman turned to talk to him.

She had a deformed face, her tangled hair fell to her shoulders like fraying ropes, and her lips formed two thick lines that hid ugly teeth. Her small eyes watched him carefully. Alarmed by how ugly she was, King Arthur couldn't look at her.

"I am Lady Ragnell," the woman said. "I know what you are looking for, Your Majesty, and I can save your life, but on one condition."

King Arthur had a hard time paying attention, so distracted by her appearance as he was. Yet nothing could be worse than to lose his life at the hands of Sir Gromer, so he forced himself to listen. He nodded at the woman to continue.

"I'll tell you what women want," she said simply, "if Sir Gawain agrees to marry me."

The frightening woman's words weren't a threat. She wasn't speaking angrily, but with sadness and resignation.

In truth, she was a sorceress, and she was pinning all her hopes for her future happiness on King Arthur's answer. The king, however, could only see the woman's ugly features and didn't want to burden his nephew with an unhappy marriage. To give himself time to think, he told Lady Ragnell that he would need to ask Sir Gawain for his thoughts on the matter, and he rode back to the castle.

When the king met up with Sir Gawain, he hesitated to tell his nephew what had transpired in the forest. But the younger man wanted to know what the sorceress had proposed.

"I don't need to think it over," Sir Gawain responded when King Arthur told him the full story. "I will of course marry her if it saves your life."

King Arthur didn't want to condemn his nephew to such a marriage, but he recognized Lady Ragnell's offer as his only chance of survival. With a heavy heart, he got back on his horse and returned to the forest.

"Do you have Sir Gawain's answer?" the sorceress asked as the king rode up to the spot where he had left her.

Looking into the woman's ugly eyes, the king nodded. Yes, he told her, his nephew would marry her.

Having gotten what she wanted, Lady Ragnell smiled strangely and blurted out the answer the king had been seeking for a year. "Women want the freedom to decide things for themselves," she told him.

King Arthur recalled all the answers the women in the kingdom had given him and realized that Lady Ragnell had answered well, expressing the thing that all the answers he and Gawain had obtained had in common. Armed with this knowledge, the king bowed his head goodbye, dug his spurs into his horse, and set off to find Sir Gromer in the middle of the forest.

When the Knight of the Black Armor heard King Arthur's reply, his face balled up into an ugly grimace.

"Curses!" he roared. "Only my sister, Lady Ragnell, could have given you that answer."

Upon hearing that, King Arthur felt as if a fiery lance had struck his heart. If this sorceress was the sister of Sir Gromer Somer Joure, not only had he fallen into a trap, but worse, he had pulled his nephew into it as well. He had to find a way to block the marriage!

He hurried back to the castle and revealed the horrible truth to Sir Gawain.

"I appreciate your warning," his nephew answered, "but I will still keep my end of the bargain. I have given my word."

While preparations were made for the wedding, King Arthur tried repeatedly to get his nephew to change his mind, but to no avail.

Finally, the day that Lady Ragnell had been waiting for—and that King Arthur had been dreading—arrived. The ceremony was held at the edge of the forest. The bride arrived with her face covered by a veil, which she kept securely in place until the day ended and the newlyweds were finally alone.

Lady Ragnell took off her veil, and Sir Gawain, having heard what his uncle had said about her appearance, tried not to look at her. After a few moments, though, he realized that, if he was going to share the rest of his life with Lady Ragnell, he should treat her kindly. No matter how ugly her face, this young woman had saved his uncle's life; she had done nothing to deserve such contempt.

With these thoughts running through his mind, Sir Gawain approached his new wife and gave her a heartfelt kiss, hoping that one day it would be sincere. As his lips touched her deformed face, Lady Ragnell felt her heart opening up, and a tear trickled down her cheek. As that happened, her ugliness disappeared and she transformed into a beautiful young woman.

Sir Gawain could hardly believe his eyes. Before he could ask her what had happened, Lady Ragnell revealed the truth.

"I have lived for years under a horrible spell that gave me the face you saw," she explained. "My brother, Sir Gromer, believed that I had to help him cast his spells because I was a woman. When I refused to help him, he cursed me. Only if a good-hearted knight agreed to marry me, despite my appearance, would the curse begin to break."

Sir Gawain listened carefully to his wife's words, amazed by her transformation. But Lady Ragnell kept talking. She said that only half the spell

had been broken with the kiss. *How can I break the second half?* Sir Gawain wondered. As if Lady Ragnell had read his mind, she began answering the question he had not posed aloud.

"The spell dictates that I can only be beautiful half the time," Lady Ragnell explained. "You can choose for me to have this pretty face during the day alone, and all the people of the kingdom will see me as you see me now. Or you can choose to have me look pretty only at night, when you and I are alone together. Which would you prefer?"

As she spoke, Sir Gawain couldn't stop thinking about how difficult a decision this was. He glanced tenderly at Lady Ragnell. *She is brave, wise, and beautiful*, he thought.

Sir Gawain took his wife's hands into his and said, "You should be the one to decide what you want. I will always be by your side, no matter what you look like."

"Do you give me the freedom to choose my own fate?" Lady Ragnell asked, holding back her emotions.

"Only you control your fate," answered Sir Gawain. "You are free to decide your own life, just as a bird decides whether to fly or stay on a branch."

Lady Ragnell gazed at her husband for a long time. Without knowing it, he had said exactly the right words to break the curse completely; she was free. As Sir Gawain spoke, Lady Ragnell recovered her original beautiful face forever, day and night. The young couple's romance, born out of freedom, was perfect.

The Female
Head of the Family

A Tale from China

Many years ago, there lived an old widower with his three sons. Following tradition, when the two oldest sons married, their wives, Xia and Lian, came to live in their husbands' house. Custom usually required the wives to ask their mother-in-law for permission when they wanted to visit their own mothers, but since the widower's wife had died a long time ago, Xia and Lian had to ask their father-in-law for permission instead.

As the two wives were young and greatly missed their maternal homes, they requested permission to visit quite often. Their father-in-law, an old man with a strong personality and very little patience, grew increasingly upset as this went on. After years of working hard, he had looked forward to the peace and quiet that came with old age, and the constant requests wore at him.

Frustrated, the old man finally turned to his daughters-in-law and said, "You're always asking me for permission to visit your mothers. Please don't do this anymore; I'd much rather you leave me alone. Whenever you come to me to ask about these visits, I act rude and self-centered out of frustration, and yet I would hate to offend you."

The old man told them that, from that day onward, they could go visit their mothers whenever they wanted, without asking for permission, under one condition: "You must bring me things I have always wanted: a fistful of flames and a handful of wind."

Xia and Lian looked at each other almost in tears. What their father-in-law asked for was impossible.

"If you promise to bring me what I ask for, you can come and go as you please," he said. And then he added, "But if you don't keep your word, you will never be able to return to your childhood homes."

What the old man really wanted was to discourage his daughters-in-law so that they would no longer bother him and he could live his life in peace. What he hadn't considered, though, was the youthful vigor and courage possessed by Xia and Lian. As they heard the old man speaking, the two women's hearts were awakened to the idea of breaking with this unjust tradition, one that was not only unfair but that was now impacting their lives as well. They both accepted the challenge, promising to satisfy his wish upon their return.

With that, Xia and Lian quickly got ready for their journey and took the road to their respective homes, their father-in-law's request already only a passing thought in their minds.

While resting under a tree along the way, Xia sighed. "I was so excited to see my mother that I didn't stop to think that I might never see my husband ever again," she said. For she feared that, if they turned up empty-handed, her father-in-law would bar them from his home.

"The same thing happened to me," Lian said. "I would've agreed to almost any request placed upon us by our father-in-law if it meant seeing my mother, but what he asks for is impossible."

Just then, a young woman named Min, who had been traveling down the same road, stopped to talk to them. She noticed how upset they were and asked what was wrong. The brides had such a strong need to vent that they shared their dilemma with a stranger. They were not seeking help, but when Min offered to assist them, the girls gladly accepted.

"We have nothing to lose," they decided, and so the three women went on their way together.

Min took them to her home, where she lived with her father. She cooked a soup to relax them and explained the simple way they could fulfill their father-in-law's demands.

"A paper lantern is a fistful of flames," Min said. This brilliant answer surprised Xia and Lian. What had seemed impossible was simply a matter of imagination.

"As for the handful of wind," Min went on, "just bring him a fan and shake it in his face."

Xia and Lian continued on their way in the morning, anxious to reunite with their families. After spending several days with their mothers, they knew the time had come to return to their husbands, whom they loved very much.

When Xia and Lian returned with assurances that they had met their father-in-law's demands, the old man was surprised—to his mind, what he had asked for was impossible. Not so, said the two women.

"Here's your handful of wind," Xia said, fanning her father-in-law with a fan she had brought from home.

Lian then lit the paper lantern she had acquired and placed it near the old man so he could feel the warmth of the flames. "And here is your fistful of fire," she said.

The old man, surprised by their cleverness, agreed that his daughters-in-law had kept their promises. From that moment on, they could come and go as they pleased without permission. The young women were grateful and wanted to further please the old man, so they told him about Min.

"She's a clever woman," they noted. "Despite her youth, she, not her father, is in charge of their house."

Upon hearing this, the old man asked to meet Min, thinking she would be the perfect wife for his youngest son, Qiang.

After some time, the women arranged a meeting, and the old man and Qiang went for a visit. Min, a strong young woman, was practical and industrious, and she was so absorbed by her work that she had never given a thought to love. But the moment she met Qiang, fate intervened, and the two young people fell in love. Qiang's and Min's fathers were both pleased, since tradition insisted that they find a wife for the son and a husband for the daughter, and they all blessed the union. After a short courtship, the couple married, and Min moved home to live with Qiang, under his father's roof.

After this wedding, the old man gathered all the household members and declared his new rule. "From now on," he said, "Min will be the head of the family. I am too old to continue. You must obey her and do whatever she commands."

The family gladly welcomed Min, who immediately got to work. She told the family to water the land each time they went into the fields, and also asked them to bring back a bundle of kindling whenever they returned. By following these instructions carefully, the family was able to have the best harvest they'd had in years, and they could cook and heat their house as well, all with little effort. When the fields needed no water and the house needed no kindling, rather than letting them laze about, Min had the family drag back large stones from a nearby quarry, which she knew they could use to make their house bigger. Soon enough, they had accumulated a large pile.

One day, an expert in precious gems was walking past and saw a piece of jade among the rocks. Without mentioning the jade, he offered the family a large sum of money for the entire pile of rocks. The men of the house were pleased with his offer, but Min was unsure. She asked herself why this stranger would want to pay so much money for a heap of jagged stones. Though he had said he wanted to build his own house, she suspected that this was not as good a bargain as it had first appeared.

Min decided to invite the man for dinner, and she gave her family instructions to ply him with wine and get him to talk a lot. She told them she wanted to suss out the reason behind his offer.

And her plan was successful: during dinner, as the man spoke, Min came to understand that he had found a precious gem among the rocks. Quietly, she asked her husband to go through all the stones until he found the valuable gem. When he located it, he handed it over to Min, who hid the jade and returned to the conversation, planning to close the deal the stranger had proposed.

"Sir, if our stones are so good for building," Min said, "we should set a more just price. I think you should pay us twice what you have offered."

The stranger, anxious to gain possession of the jade, did not argue. He paid the higher amount and took away the pile of rough stones, not knowing that the jade had been removed. Since he had not negotiated honestly, he could not complain once he discovered what Min had done. The man kept the pile of jagged stones, upset that he had underestimated the young head of the family.

"In the end, the joke is on me," he said to himself.

Thanks to Min, the family grew richer and richer. Not only did they have the money the stranger had paid, but because they now had the jade, they also amassed greater wealth. They built a luxurious palace, and in the front, they set a flagstone above the door upon which was inscribed the saying: *No worries.*

In a short time, the family's wealth became known throughout the region. One day, out of mere curiosity, a magistrate visited with his entourage. He wanted to see whether the rumors of the family's riches were true or simply idle talk. When he arrived and saw the truth behind what he'd heard, he became so jealous that even the inscription upset him.

"I wish to speak to the head of the family," he declared.

When young Min came to the door in answer, the magistrate and his entourage gasped. "Are you the head of the family?"

Min nodded.

"You are a strange family," the magistrate objected. "Not only because a young lady is your head, but also because you have a presumptuous inscription above your door. Are you unaware of the suffering of others?"

"Worries and sadness serve no purpose, sir," Min said. "That's why you will not find them in this house."

"How arrogant," the magistrate replied, upset by Min's sharp response. "You deserve to be punished. Give me a piece of cloth as long as this path."

"We will begin weaving once Your Excellency tells us where the path starts and ends," Min responded.

Angered by the answer, the magistrate increased the punishment. "You must also give me as much oil as there is water in the ocean."

"We will begin to extract the oil, Your Highness," Min answered, "once you tell us just how much water there is in the ocean."

The magistrate, fed up with her answers, grimaced. "If you are so smart," he huffed, "why don't you tell me what I am thinking? See this pheasant in my hand? Tell me if I want to kill it or set it free. I won't fine you if you tell me what I'm thinking."

"You are an eminent, cultured person, sir. You know much more than I do," Min responded. "So if I have one foot inside and the other outside the house, am I going in or coming out?"

At that, the magistrate realized that Min was a very unusual young woman. Without a moment's hesitation, she had given him clever and thoughtful responses to his questions. It was clear to him now that her intelligence and cleverness deserved his full respect.

He turned around and ordered his entourage to leave the palace grounds. "This young woman deserves to be left in peace," he declared, "so that her great cleverness will continue to bring happiness and good fortune, not only to her family, but also to the rest of the region."

Min lived as head of the family's household for many years, and in time, she did just that.

The Female Warrior

A Tale from Spain

I n a never-ending war between two neighboring king-doms, first the young men from each realm came to the battlefront. When there were no young men left to fight, their fathers took up their swords, and after that, their grandfathers as well. Neither army seemed strong enough to win the gru-eling war.

In the midst of it all, old Don Martin cursed his bad luck at not being able to help his king in battle. Not only was he too old to grip a sword, but worse, he had no son. He cursed his bad luck at having six daughters.

One day, Don Martin's youngest daughter heard her father complaining about his misfortune. "If only I had one son to go off to war!" the old man sobbed.

Jimena was a determined young woman, with great willpower and a strong character. She felt a special affection for her father. She set herself to thinking of what might cheer him up.

"Father," she declared, "I want to go off to war. I need only dress up like a man, then I could serve the king disguised as your son."

At first, Don Martin rejected such an absurd idea. He thought such a thing would be impossible! But when his daughter insisted, he reconsidered. Could she really dress up as a man and fool the king's armies?

"I admire your courage," the old man said, "but I'm afraid your plan won't work. Men's clothes simply aren't made for women's bodies."

Jimena reassured her father: she would tie a cloth tightly around her chest so she would resemble a man and be able to wear men's clothing.

"But, daughter," Don Martin added, "your white hands, delicate as the wings of doves, will give you away. The only people I know with hands like yours are women."

Once more Jimena showed her great determination. Before going to war, she would let the sun brown her hands, and she would do hard work to strengthen them. Although her father wasn't entirely convinced, he listened to her more carefully now. As he gave it more thought, he realized: her idea didn't seem so far-fetched after all.

But before he could fully agree to Jimena's plan, he expressed one final doubt. "Dear daughter," he reminded her, "your beautiful hair that reflects the sunlight and glitters so beautifully at night would give you away, for most people would see it as the hair of a woman."

"I can rub coal dust into my hair, Father," she explained, "and it will look so messy that no one will know who I am. Don't worry. Not only can I defend myself, I can also defend our king." And with that it was determined: Jimena would go off to war.

Only one thing had to be decided before she left: What would she call herself?

"Don Martin," her father began. "Don Martin of Aragon! Nothing would fill me with more pride than having you carry my name."

And so Don Martin's name and Jimena's ingenuity hid the young woman as she went to battle. Not a single person discovered her true identity, as Jimena was fearless and courageous, fighting shoulder to shoulder with the other soldiers. Even off the battlefield, she continued her pretense of being a man, and so no one found her out. Through it all, only Jimena's eyes remained the same, reflecting her unique way of seeing the world. Her eyes, she knew, were the only part of her that might reveal her secret.

For two years, "Don Martin of Aragon" fought side by side with the king's son. In time, they formed a deep friendship, and one day, when the prince looked into Jimena's eyes, he realized he was in love.

"I am tormented by the love I feel," the prince confessed to his mother, the queen. "My heart beats faster when I look at Don Martin's eyes. I swear they are a woman's eyes, but how can that be?"

The queen listened to her son tenderly. She considered herself well versed in both the desires and the weaknesses of women, and so she gave him her best advice. "Son, in order to learn the truth, you must take Don Martin to the market," she told him. "If he is a woman, he will pause at the fabric stands, since most women like to imagine new dresses."

Following his mother's suggestion, the prince took Don Martin to the market the next day. Jimena, however, had never been interested in dresses. In fact, while pretending to be a man, she had discovered a love of hunting, and so, when she and the prince reached the market, she went directly to the stand where hunting gear was sold, and expressed her pleasure at seeing a live falcon.

This wasn't what the prince had expected. Yet he was still convinced that Don Martin was somehow a woman.

The queen proposed another test to unveil the truth. "Take her to the palace gardens; I know I could never be indifferent to the smell of jasmine and orange blossoms," she told her son.

So the next afternoon, when the sun was particularly hot and the garden flowers smelled their most fresh and sweet, the prince and Don Martin went for a stroll. Jimena, who wasn't enamored of nature, expressed her deep love of architecture as they walked. She remarked upon the height and thickness of the palace walls, admiring the bulk of the columns. She asked question upon question about how the palace had been constructed.

Neither of the queen's tests had proven that Don Martin was a woman, but the prince was still intrigued. It wasn't only Don Martin's eyes that enticed the prince; it was also how he spoke, elegantly and intelligently. The prince knew that he and Don Martin shared the same interests, and, most important, they both desired an end to the war. The prince was determined to get to the bottom of Don Martin's secret.

"Mother, I am as sure that Don Martin is a woman as I am that night follows day," he insisted.

The queen saw that her son was upset, so she suggested one more test. "Why don't you go to an inn and suggest spending the night in the same bed?" his mother offered. "If Don Martin is a woman, she would likely refuse, to save her honor."

The prince did what his mother proposed, but once again to no conclusion. Jimena noted how cold the room was, and slept in the bed fully clothed.

The prince spent the night awake, listening to Don Martin's soft breathing. *I've never seen a man sleep like that*, he thought to himself, *with so much sweetness perched on his closed lids.*

As time went on, the prince fell even more deeply in love. Though he could clearly see that Don Martin's words and gestures were those of the male soldiers he'd known, he was convinced that there was a woman behind those eyes.

"Take her to a river to go swimming with the other soldiers," the queen said, attempting to come up with one last test. "Then you might know whether Don Martin is a man or a woman."

As the other soldiers took off their uniforms and boots at the river's edge, Jimena realized she was in a bind. She would have to either confess her secret or leave the battlefield forever. Not wanting to bring shame to her father's name, she gathered her belongings and, with a heavy heart, got up on her horse.

She rode over to the prince and caught his attention. "I've just received a letter that my father is ill," she lied. "Might I have your leave to go home and see him?"

The prince immediately gave his permission. Whether Don Martin was a man or a woman was irrelevant; he would not stop someone from going to help a parent in need.

Jimena saw the kindness in the prince's heart and realized that she was in love with him, but, of course, there was no way that she saw fit to tell him who she truly was. Instead, she just galloped away from the river shore, on her way back home.

The prince stood and watched Don Martin gallop away, thinking hard about how he might find out the truth and act on his love. Suddenly, a thought occurred to him: he had forgotten to say goodbye! Without any further thought, he mounted his horse and raced after the departing soldier.

Just as he was about to catch up with Don Martin, he heard the voice of a young woman speaking aloud. "Goodbye, Prince," she said sadly. "Don Martin begs his leave. You will never know that a woman fought the enemy at your side."

As she said those words, Jimena heard the sound of galloping hooves behind her. She glanced back and saw the prince, and, with tears in her eyes, realized that he had heard her, that he knew the truth. But although she was sad to be leaving behind a friend, perhaps even a love, she knew that they were fated to part, and so she spurred her horse and rode home without stopping or looking back at all.

When she arrived, her old father received her with open arms. "You've returned safe and sound," he sobbed. "I give thanks to God!"

Jimena greeted him with a warm embrace. "Father, you warned me about all the different ways people might discover the truth," she said. "But I never gave myself away, and fighting on the battle's front lines kept anyone from suspecting me."

Her father looked at her, bursting with pride.

As they spoke, they heard the sound of a horse and rider. Looking toward the gate, Jimena was amazed to see the prince! It seemed he had followed Jimena all the way to her father's home and had heard much of her conversation with the real Don Martin.

He came up alongside the young woman and her father, then dismounted and approached the two. "I fell in love with the goodness of the soldier I knew as Don Martin," he said. "And now I have fallen in love with the bravery and courage of you, Jimena."

Certain at last that his love was a woman, he professed his devotion to her, and she confessed her love in return. The couple embraced, free of secrets at last.

The Prince
and the Three Fates

A Tale from Egypt

housands of years ago, Egypt's pharaoh brought together all his priests and priestesses to bless his son, the crown prince, on the day of his birth. As the priests gathered around the royal cradle, their smiles turned slowly into grimaces.

"What's wrong?" asked the queen, alarmed.

"An unhappy fate awaits your son," said the youngest priestess. "There's nothing we can do for him. It's been foretold that a dog, a snake, or a crocodile will kill him."

The pharaoh and his wife were so upset by the prophecy that they ordered a castle to be built for their son, to save him from the fate that awaited him.

In the months that followed, a fortified palace was built. The pharaoh's architects and builders worked tirelessly to replicate the royal grounds down to the smallest detail. When it was done, it became the young prince's refuge.

And so the young crown prince grew up surrounded by toys, nannies, and people to entertain him. At night, guards walked the grounds to make sure no dog, snake, or crocodile could come near.

One day, as the little prince walked along the walls of the fortress, he saw something in the distant desert that drew his attention.

"What's that?" he asked, full of curiosity.

His nanny explained to him that it was a dog, something nasty and dangerous. Still, the little boy was intrigued and wanted to play with it. Since his nanny would not let him, he went to talk to his father.

The pharaoh had dreaded the moment when he would have to explain to his son the omen regarding his fate.

"It's been prophesized that a dog, a snake, or a crocodile will kill you," his father told him. "That's why you should stay away from that dog."

The crown prince, however, was not scared. On the contrary, he was greatly relieved to finally understand why he had been raised in isolation in the palace. At that moment, he decided he did not want to live his life in fear.

"Father," he said, "I want that dog to accompany me. I am very unhappy being alone here."

The pharaoh, seeing his son's loneliness and thinking that one small dog couldn't hurt his son, gave in. A few days later, he gave his son a puppy that licked and nibbled him affectionately.

The years went by without the future king tasting danger. As time passed, and the prince grew to be a man, he became tired of living locked up within the palace walls. He wasn't afraid of anything; he had been trained to fight off all kinds of beasts. Why, then, should he be afraid of an old prophecy?

He begged his father to let him go, for he desired nothing more than to be free. He wanted to travel all over the world—only by traveling would he be able to rule Egypt with the wisdom and temperance of a pharaoh. For peace of mind, he would go forth with the dog that had been with him

since childhood. The dog was now fully grown—he was ferocious and would attack anything that threatened his master.

The pharaoh understood what his son wanted and let him go. "If your future comes back looking for you, it will be harder for it to find you if you are not here or in any part of Egypt," he said. "I will buy a boat for you to sail up the Nile so the future can never find you."

So the prince climbed atop his horse, said goodbye to his father, and galloped to the harbor, where he and his dog boarded a ship setting sail for Aswan province. After a few weeks on board, the prince glimpsed the flag of a far-off kingdom on the coast of the Red Sea. It seemed a good place to start a new life, one where he could overcome his fate and where no one would know about his royal blood.

Upon his arrival, the young man discovered that this kingdom was ruled by a just and merciful king, of whom everyone spoke highly. The king had a beloved daughter for whom he had recently built a magnificent palace, complete with the tallest minaret in the whole kingdom. It was seventy feet tall and had seventy windows, and it was meant to attract a prince deserving of his daughter. She was the prize for the young man able to climb up to the window by which the princess waited.

At that moment, a royal messenger was traveling to neighboring kingdoms to announce the king's challenge. The princess approved of it—in fact, it would save her from having to talk to all the boring, self-centered suitors who were sure to try to win her hand. The virtues she most admired were prudence and intelligence, and the king's challenge wasn't for impetuous, foolish young men, especially since the palace walls were of made of marble that was as smooth as glass.

Each morning, after finishing her chores, the future queen sat by the window and saw dozens of young men showing off—running, leaping, and climbing, only to crash back to the ground, cursing their bad luck.

All kinds of people came to the palace walls: not just climbers, but also locals who enjoyed seeing the palace's white walls splashed with the dazzling array of colors provided by those who were attempting the challenge. Though some suitors managed to climb high up, no one could reach the window by which the princess waited.

As days went by, the number of suitors grew and grew, and the prince decided to try his luck as well. He went to see the palace. When he reached the designated wall, instead of jumping immediately as many others had done, only to fail, he first stopped to study what the other suitors did. Thus the prince learned which parts of the wall were most difficult to scale and which parts to avoid. He memorized the cracks and protrusions, no matter how small. He learned from the mistakes of others, and when he finally felt ready, he began to climb. Knowing by heart which path to take, he surprised the onlookers with his speed and dexterity, especially when he reached the princess's windowsill in a matter of minutes.

"I have been watching you study the others for days," the princess said in greeting. "I knew that because of your caution and cleverness you would make it all the way up."

The young prince and princess continued to converse, and after a short while, they fell in love. As the news spread through the kingdom that a young man had successfully climbed the wall, the king was comforted, for he had feared that no young man would succeed. But his happiness turned to anger when he discovered the man was not a prince but a commoner.

"He must leave my kingdom immediately!" ordered the king. "How dare he try to court my daughter? She is a princess, after all!"

He gave orders to arrest the young man, have him placed in a dungeon, and have him executed the next day for his impertinence.

"Father, please consider what the people will think of a king who breaks his promise," the princess whispered. "You never said that the contender had to be of royal blood."

The princess's wise words calmed the king, and he summoned the young man to his throne room.

"Tell me who you are," the king demanded when the prince arrived. "Hearing you speak makes it difficult for me to think that you are a commoner."

"My mother tutored me," the young man answered, not wanting to reveal his identity to the king for fear his fate would find him.

The king reluctantly accepted this explanation and blessed the marriage. Before the ceremony, the young man wanted to share the truth with his future wife.

"I am a prince, but my life is in the hands of one of three creatures—a crocodile, a snake, or a dog," he confessed.

The princess listened to the story of the prophecy, and when it was done, she found herself confused. If a dog was likely to kill him, how could the prince have so much affection for his own pet?

"He's been my companion since childhood," the prince replied. "He would never hurt me. Don't worry, I will always carry a sword with me. And whenever I leave the palace, I will be accompanied by royal guards."

The young couple married the following day.

Months later, news arrived that a lonely, ailing pharaoh was searching for his son, the crown prince, to spend the last days of his life with him.

The young man decided to visit his father and fulfill his dying wish. He said goodbye to his wife and began the long journey home. When the prince was reunited with his elderly father in Egypt, he realized how much he had missed his home, and he knew he could not leave again. He asked his wife to join him so that they could rule together.

One night, while the princess struggled to sleep, she saw a strange creature in the corner of their bedroom. Its eyes glowed in the darkness, and it moved slowly toward her husband, who was sleeping peacefully. Frightened, she shrank back, realizing she was seeing a huge snake—one of the creatures from the prophecy.

Regaining her courage, she quickly came up with a plan. She placed a mirror and a bowl of hot milk on the floor. Attracted by the smell, the snake crept up to the bowl of milk. When it saw its reflection in the nearby mirror, it thought that another snake was also slithering around, trying to steal its food. The creature struggled with its reflection until it collapsed in exhaustion. Thanks to the princess, the prince was able to escape the first of his three fates.

The next morning, the young man rode on horseback to the river, followed by his dog, who was so old now that his vision had started to fail him. As they traveled, the dog barked, having seen something that looked like a tree trunk. The prince got off his horse to examine it, only to realize that he was looking at the huge snout of a Nile crocodile.

"You can't escape from me," said the reptile. "I am your fate."

The prince made a hasty retreat and realized that, no matter what he did, he would always be under the same threat of death. For the first time in his life, he was afraid, and so he went to visit an old wizard and seek his advice.

"There's one way to escape this prophecy," the wizard told him. "You must dig a hole in the dry sand and fill it with water. Only by doing this can you destroy the prophecy's power. Otherwise, you will soon die."

The young men left the wizard full of distress, knowing full well that it was impossible to keep water inside a sand hole. He shared his worries with the princess, who saw how dejected he was. She, too, realized this was a strange, impossible task.

"How can a sand hole remain filled with water?" the young man asked.

"Don't worry," the princess said, calming him. "I have studied plants. In the desert not too far from here is a flower with thirteen petals that can ensure that water will stay in a sand hole for as long as a year. In the morning, I will go fetch it. Meanwhile, you can begin digging the hole."

Just before the sun rose the next morning, the princess headed out to the desert. Her heart beat nervously, as she was not entirely certain that she could find the right flower. As she rode, she met a sacred cat representing Bastet, the Egyptian goddess of harmony and happiness, who offered to help her. The cat told her that she could find the magic flower at the top of the mountain where the winds of the angry gods blew.

The princess approached the mountain and began climbing to the top, grabbing on to the smallest crevices in the stone with her fingertips. "If my husband could climb our castle walls without knowing me, surely I can climb this mountain to save the life of a man who I know and love," she said to herself.

When she finally reached the mountaintop, a windstorm began blowing, forcing her to close her eyes. Though she wasn't able to find the flower quickly or easily, she didn't give up; instead, she knelt on the ground and felt all around with her hands until her fingers brushed a very delicate flower that was growing in the crevice between two rocks. She trembled as she counted the petals: one, two, three . . . all the way to thirteen. Overjoyed at finding the right one, she placed the flower inside her blouse and began her climb back down the mountain.

When she returned home, she found her husband at the river's edge, next to the hole he had dug. The crocodile he had narrowly escaped from was there, his eyes fixed on the prince. The princess placed the flower in the hole, and the prince poured the water and waited. A few minutes passed, and then an hour, and still the water hadn't drained. The princess looked triumphantly at the crocodile, who then vanished into the river.

And so, thanks to the princess, the prince was able to escape the second of his fates.

The happy couple celebrated their luck by going to a nearby marsh. As usual, the prince's faithful dog accompanied him. By now, the old dog's vision had worsened to the point where he could barely see, and as they walked, he fell into a swampy hole. Without a moment's thought, the prince leapt into the hole to try to save his beloved pet, but the waters were treacherous, and before long, the dog began to sink. The princess, thinking quickly to prevent her husband from sinking as well, found a rope, tossed it to him, and pulled him out of the water. The prince survived, but he was unable to save his dog.

"I'm so sorry your dog has died," the princess cried, feeling her husband's pain. "But at least now you won't have to worry about your future."

And that was how the princess's wisdom, courage, and strength allowed the prince to be freed from his terrible fate.

Mulha
and the Imbula

A Swazi Tale from Southern Africa

any years ago in the kingdom of Swazi, between South Africa and Mozambique, there was a village in which a young Bantu girl named Mulha lived with her father, mother, and two younger siblings. Their house was part of a remote kraal, a group of huts that formed a peaceful circle. They hardly ever saw strangers, since they lived in the middle of a poor, dry land. Mulha's father traveled a long distance each day to reach a fertile valley where he farmed a plot of land. Sometimes, during the harvest, he would be away from home for several weeks. At those times, his children missed him greatly.

One year, during the early spring, the father grabbed his hoe and went to the valley to plant corn. He said a special goodbye to his children, for he knew he would be gone for a long time. A few days later, their mother also went to work in the fields. She asked Mulha to take care of her little siblings while she was gone. The mother left enough corn and wheat for them to eat, and she warned them not to open the huge pot in the back of the hut.

"If you behave while I am gone, we'll slaughter a goat upon my return and throw a big party," their mother said. "You can invite all your friends over to celebrate."

The children behaved well for several days. They milked the goats, made cheese, ground the corn, baked bread, and even lit fires, which they fed with manure. But after a while, Mulha's siblings missed their parents and were bored of being alone. They asked Mulha to open the pot in the back of the hut.

It broke the young girl's heart to hear her siblings pleading, and, though she knew she shouldn't, she decided to please them. When she uncovered the pot, an inzimu, a huge ogre, appeared.

The ogre's body was so big that it filled the entire hut. Mulha and her brother fled in terror, but the inzimu spoke so softly and sweetly that they lost their fear and returned.

"Don't worry. I won't hurt you," he assured them. "On the contrary. I want to make you a delicious dinner. Why don't you two go out and get me water? I will stay here with your baby sister and make sure the fire stays lit."

Mulha and her brother grabbed a few bowls and went to look for water. As soon as they were out of sight and the inzimu was alone with their younger sister, the ogre scooped her up and hid her away, planning to cook her for dinner later.

When the two older children returned, they noticed that their younger sister was missing.

"Where's our little sister?" Mulha asked.

"She's gone out to get manure for the fire," the inzimu lied. "She'll be back soon."

The ogre also planned to fatten the two older children. When they were nice and plump, he would eat them, too. So the inzimu put big plates in front of the children for dinner. But just then, a bee started buzzing around them.

"Don't eat anything. It's all a trap," the bee whispered. "While you were out, the ogre took your sister and hid her."

Alerted by the bee, Mulha and her brother refused to eat. As night fell, they went to the back of the hut and curled up, plotting their escape. As soon as the inzimu fell asleep, they found where the ogre had hidden their sister and rescued her. Then the three of them ran off as fast as they could. But just as they started to feel safe, the inzimu appeared on the path before them.

"Where are you going?" he asked, hiding his anger.

Mulha hid their younger sister behind her back. "Oh, we're going to play by the river," she and her brother answered calmly.

They walked quickly, hurrying toward the gurgling water, hoping to escape before the inzimu figured out what they were doing. But they weren't fast enough: the ogre realized they were trying to escape and ran after them. He caught Mulha, who had purposely been lagging behind so that her siblings would have time to hide in the bushes growing along the riverbanks.

In the meantime, her siblings reached the river. Seeing that Mulha had been caught, they went off in search of their mother, who they hoped would come to save them. They swam and swam until they reached the field where she was working.

The ogre, not satisfied with just Mulha, went looking for her brother as well, and Mulha saw her opportunity to escape. Running away, she was able to reach her mother and explain what had happened. Her mother, hearing all that had transpired, knew that the inzimu would go back to the hut and that none of them would be safe; she knew that Mulha especially would be in danger, since she had devised the escape plan.

"Go live with your aunt," her mother told her. "She is married and has a good job. She will take care of you and help you find a husband."

So Mulha washed herself in the river, put on a pretty dress, and tied a blue-and-green sash around her waist. Then she beaded several necklaces and placed them around her neck. Before Mulha left, her mother gave her one last piece of advice: stay on the path and let nothing distract her. "Don't touch the manumbela tree," she warned. "Its shiny leaves and silver trunk will tempt you. Whatever you do, don't eat its red berries."

Her mother watched her leave, proud of how her daughter walked with such freedom and determination to her new destiny. She was convinced that soon she would marry a tribal chief's son.

Mulha walked for a very long time, so long that the sun burned her skin and she felt more tired and thirsty with each step. She looked around, but did not find water or anything else that could quench her thirst. She walked on and on until she felt exhausted, and just as she was about to lose all hope, she saw a beautiful manumbela tree. She could almost taste its juicy fruit. She got closer, hoping to rest in the shade of its leaves, and thinking about how many hours it had been since she'd had water to drink and how parched her throat had become. As soon as Mulha touched the berries, though, before she had even put them in her mouth, the tree trunk split in two and an imbula, a horrible female ogress with a wolf's snout and hairy body as well as a long tail, came out from inside.

"Beautiful Bantu girl, it's not safe to travel alone," the imbula said. "Give me your clothes and your necklaces. You can wear my skin—that way no one will recognize you, and you can continue on your way without danger."

Mulha wasn't sure this was such a good idea, but since the imbula was so certain, she gave the creature her pretty dress as well as her green-and-blue sash. She also gave her several of the beaded necklaces, keeping just one as a remembrance.

"You should give me all your necklaces," the imbula insisted. "Otherwise you might draw attention. When you are safe, I will return them all to you."

Mulha gave in and handed over her final necklace, and then put on the ogress's skin. Her disguise worked: nobody stopped her on her journey, and soon she approached the river near her aunt's kraal. There, she once again encountered the imbula, who, dressed in Mulha's clothes and no longer looking monstrous, would be welcomed by her mother's sister with great affection.

Scared, Mulha tried to take off the ogress's rags and the wolf's snout, but they were glued to her body as if they were her own skin. The imbula, on the other hand, seemed more beautiful than ever: her teeth were as white as marble, her skin as silky and shiny as a bird-of-paradise flower, her eyes glowing like two torches in the night. The real Mulha had been transformed into a repugnant monster, and the hideous ogress was now a beautiful Bantu girl.

Mulha was frightened, desperate to have her old appearance returned to her. Nervously, she tried to convince the imbula to reverse their trade, but the imbula refused repeatedly, even as they reached the aunt's village. When the two arrived, Mulha's relatives welcomed the imbula, thinking she was their niece. Mulha tried to tell her aunt and the rest of the villagers what had happened, but no one believed her. Instead, everyone simply laughed.

"Dear Mulha, tell me how we can get rid of your horrible companion," the aunt said to the ogress.

"Don't worry about her. Just leave her with the dogs," the imbula answered. "She'll be fine with them."

But Mulha's aunt preferred to leave her with an old woman who lived in a hut outside the village, thinking that she would be better off there than with the dogs. And, the aunt reasoned, sending the ogress to the old woman meant that she would no longer be alone in her old age.

Thus, the imbula settled into the kraal; she was so beautiful that everyone treated her like a princess. Her only worry was about her tail, since she had no magic potion to hide it. Every day, she rolled it around her waist and hid it under her clothing, always afraid that it would be discovered. But time went by, and no one ever saw it.

Meanwhile, the real Mulha, imprisoned in her ogress skin, lived in the old woman's shack and took care of her. She felt enormously sad that her aunt had treated her so poorly. As time passed, though, she slowly discovered that the ogress's skin had magical powers, and she began to learn how to use them.

The first thing she discovered was that these magical powers could bring her delicious fruits and vegetables—no longer did she and the old woman have to eat the food the neighbors threw out. Since they had everything they needed, they no longer needed to beg.

"Tell me," Mulha said to the old woman one day, "would you like to be young again?"

"Of course," the old woman answered without hesitating.

The next morning, the old woman woke up young and healthy—she could scarcely believe her eyes. When the villagers saw her, they asked what had happened, but Mulha begged her to keep it a secret. She didn't want the imbula to suspect the truth: that she had learned to use the ogress's magic.

The imbula, still impersonating Mulha, had no need for her old magic. She had all the comforts she could need from Mulha's aunt, and was being introduced to several young men who hoped to marry her. But the imbula, who had become so beautiful on the outside, still had the heart of an ogress: she was lazy, selfish, and fickle. She ridiculed all her relatives and treated them with contempt. She complained about her aunt's stews and refused to help anyone, saying she needed to conserve her beauty. And beautiful she was, enough so that she caught the eye of the village chief's son, and the two were engaged.

Mulha's aunt was shocked by her niece's behavior; she was surprised to learn that the young woman had been brought up to behave in this manner. At the same time, she was curious about the ugly girl whom she had sent to live with the old woman; she had heard of the amazing things that the girl had done for other villagers, carrying firewood during the winter, farming barren lands that sprouted green plants under the burning sun, helping the weak, and being affectionate toward children.

One hot afternoon, the real Mulha went to bathe in the river. Secretly, her aunt followed her, curious to see what she might find out about the girl she still considered a mystery. The aunt's curiosity was rewarded when she saw something amazing: the moment Mulha put her foot in the water, she regained her previous appearance and was once again beautiful. The aunt could hardly believe what she'd seen, so she decided to visit a sorceress and seek her advice.

"I will go to the river with you the next time the girl goes to bathe," the sorceress suggested. "When she steps into the water, we will appear and ask her about this strange transformation."

And so it was that the next time Mulha went to the river, the sorceress and the aunt followed after her. Caught, Mulha explained the pact she had made with the imbula and revealed her true identity.

"I don't want to change my situation," she told them. "I have everything I need. When you thought I was the ugly woman, you abandoned me and accepted the imbula as your niece. So now you can continue to support her."

The aunt wasn't happy living with an ogress, no matter how pretty she was, so she went to speak to the tribal chief to see what she should do.

The tribal chief asked to hear from both Mulha and the imbula, both of whom recounted what had happened prior to their arrival at the village: Mulha told the truth, while the imbula told a story that made it seem like she had done the right thing. After hearing both Mulha's and the ogress's accounts, the tribal chief wasn't certain which of the two was accurate. She came up with a plan to find the truth.

"Dig a large hole in the middle of the village," she said. "Use a gourd to fill it with all kinds of food, and put fresh milk on top. Then each woman will walk around the hole. Soon we will know which of them is the imbula."

When the hole had been dug, Mulha walked around it many times, until the tribal chief told her to stop. When it was the imbula's turn, she refused to do it, saying that the future wife of the village chief shouldn't be treated in such a way. But the tribal chief insisted; since she had no other choice, the imbula began circling.

The imbula tried to control herself, but the smell of milk was so irresistible to the ogress that her long tail unfurled and she threw herself into the hole to drink the milk. At that moment, the tribal chief ordered her people to throw their spears at the ogress and kill her. When the first spear hit her body, she regained her original shape, and Mulha recovered her old appearance.

Having agreed to marry the imbula without knowing who she really was, the village chief's son now saw the beauty that existed in the heart of the young Bantu woman. Knowing of the kindness she had shown the old woman and the good she had done in the village, he fell immediately in love with her.

Seeing that Mulha, and not the imbula, deserved to be his son's wife, the village chief asked her to marry his son. But for the first time in her life, Mulha refused to be obliging and decided to do what her strong heart most desired. She told him that she did not want to marry yet and would never behave to please others if it went against what she truly wished. Finally free of all magic and disguise, Mulha set out to live her life exactly as she pleased.

The Barber's Wife

A Punjabi Tale from India

I n a Punjabi village many years ago, there was a barber who lamented his bad luck. Since he was a bit clumsy and his hands weren't steady, he had few customers. Those who came for shaves always left with scrapes on their cheeks; those who came for haircuts went home with nicks on their ears.

The poor man was neither skilled nor intelligent enough to find another way to make a living. As the days passed, he spent all his savings, and when he'd gone through every bit of money he had, he realized he had nothing to eat. That's when his wife, Nabiha, forced him to beg.

"One way or another you'll have to bring food into the house," she demanded, fed up with their meager life.

One day, word spread that the king was planning a luxurious party. Nabiha told her husband to go to the palace. "Surely the king will give you alms to show his generosity in front of his guests," she insisted.

The barber wasn't sure that his wife was right, but since he had no better ideas of his own, he decided to do as she said and present himself in the palace.

When he arrived, he was ushered in to meet the king, and he explained his predicament. "What can I give you?" the king asked, wanting to help.

The barber was so surprised by the question, and by the king's generosity, that all he could manage in response was to stutter that any-thing would help.

"A piece of land, perhaps?" the king asked. "It is barren, but you can try to make something grow from it."

The barber was grateful that the king had suggested something, because he had had no idea what to ask for, and he knew his wife expected him not to return empty-handed. A piece of barren land was better than nothing, he reasoned. So he accepted the king's offer.

When the barber told his wife of the king's gift, she was displeased. "And how am I supposed to buy food with a plot of land?" Nabiha complained. "We need money, not a handful of barren soil."

The barber felt he had done his duty: he had brought something back from the palace. What to do with it was up to his wife, who debated what to do next. She knew how difficult it would be to plant crops when the earth was so hard and dry that nothing would grow. She spent the whole evening and night awake; at daybreak, she came up with a solution. She woke her husband to fill him in.

"Let's go to the land the king gave you," the barber's wife began. "Whenever I say I am tired along the way, you reply: 'Just a bit longer.'"

The barber happily obeyed. He knew that his wife more than lived up to her name, Nabiha, which in Punjabi meant "intelligent." Soon they were walking over the dry, rocky land that now belonged to them.

They walked for a long time and, following Nabiha's further instructions, kept their noses to the ground, as if they were looking for something.

"Husband, I am so tired," Nabiha said every now and then.

"Just a bit longer," he replied, not lifting his eyes from the ground.

A nearby band of thieves heard Nabiha complaining. They crept up silently, watching her. Finally, sensing that they had an opportunity in front of them, the thieves approached Nabiha and asked what she was looking for.

"My husband begged me not to tell," Nabiha said to their leader, without letting on that she knew who they were, "but I'm so tired that a bit of help would do me good."

The leader of the thieves drew close to the woman so no one else could hear, and she continued to speak. "This field was my grandfather's, and somewhere here he buried a pot of gold coins," Nabiha whispered, while her husband continued walking with his eyes to the ground. "We're looking for the right spot to dig. Please, don't tell anyone."

The leader promised Nabiha that he would maintain silence even under torture. Pretending he wasn't interested in what she had just told him, he went back to his gang.

At sunset, when dark shadows raced over the land, the barber and his wife returned home. The thieves, however, had no intention of going home. They began digging—there was much land to explore and very few hours to find the pot of gold before daybreak arrived. When the sun started to rise, they were dead tired from digging all through the night, and still they hadn't found anything but tiny rocks. Exhausted, and without so much as a single coin to show for their efforts, they left the field, annoyed.

The following day, Nabiha laughed aloud when she saw the plowed land, for her plan had succeeded. With the field now ready to be planted, she went to the market hoping to find someone who might lend her a sack of rice. And because the barber's wife was known throughout the village for her intelligence, she had no trouble obtaining one from a neighbor who sold rice for a living.

"I will return this to you in triple," Nabiha promised him, and she went back to the field to plant the rice.

After months of hard work, the barber and his wife gathered the fully grown rice in a harvest more bountiful than they had dreamed of. Nabiha returned three sacks of rice to the seller, kept one sack for themselves, and sold the rest for a pot of gold coins.

When the band of thieves returned to the village and heard what had happened, they went back to Nabiha to get their share of the harvest.

"We plowed the earth," the leader said. "You must pay us for our work."

"I told you there was gold in the ground," Nabiha replied. "I didn't ask you to look for it. If you plowed the earth, well, that's your business."

The leader was furious. Powerless, he left filled with rage and making threats of revenge.

When the thieves departed, Nabiha knew they would seek their revenge that night. She decided to set a trap.

While she pretended to sleep, the thieves broke into her house to steal the pot of gold coins. Careless in their anger at Nabiha, they made so much noise that they woke the barber up.

"Hide the gold, woman!" he cried, startled, when he realized what was happening.

"Shush, don't worry," Nabiha whispered loudly. "They won't find it. The gold is in the kitchen, at the bottom of the bread basket—under the cookies, the baked bread, and the ghribat sweets."

Just as Nabiha had hoped, the thieves heard their conversation. They went into the kitchen, grabbed the basket, which included a bag of cookies that smelled of cinnamon, dates, and honey, and hurried off. When they reached their hideout, the aroma of the cookies was so strong that they devoured them as they emptied the rest of the basket, looking for the gold. It was only after they had finished the entire bag that they realized that Nabiha had added ingredients to the cookies to make them sick. For the next week, they had to stay in bed, sick to their stomachs.

When the thieves recovered, they came back to the barber's house bent on vengeance. Nabiha was expecting them, knowing that they wouldn't give up so easily. The night that they arrived, she had one eye open and, of course, a new plan in her head. Once more, the thieves entered her house making an incredible racket.

"Woman, hide the gold!" the barber yelped, waking up with the noise yet again. "Isn't it under your pillow?"

"Shush, don't worry, they won't find it," whispered Nabiha, knowing the thieves were listening. "I've taken it out of the house and placed it on the highest branch of the white acacia tree. It's safe up there."

When the thieves heard her, they went out into the garden. Since the top branch was quite high off the ground, the leader ordered one of his men to climb up and bring down the gold. What they didn't know—though, of course, Nabiha did—was that a hornet's nest, not a bag of gold, hung from the top of the tree.

The lone thief climbed halfway up the tree, pausing to rest on a branch before going any higher. As he sat there, a hornet stung him, and the man began to scratch the bite.

"What are you doing, you thug?" the other thieves shouted from the ground. "Are you trying to hide a few coins in your pocket?"

The leader of the thieves sent another man up the tree to stop the first thief from stealing. But a hornet's stinger got him as well, and when he tried to relieve the pain, his friends down below shouted: "What are you doing, you bum? A thief doesn't steal from a thief!"

The leader was angry that his men were stealing from him, and he knew the time had come to handle the matter himself. He climbed up to the top of the tree and grabbed the hornet's nest, still thinking it was the pot of gold. But when he did so, he immediately got stung and began to scratch himself just like the others.

At that point, with the three men weighing down on the tree, the acacia began to crack, and in no time at all, the branches the thieves had been sitting on broke. The three thieves fell to the ground on top of the rest of their band, and throughout the group there were broken arms, twisted legs, and bruised hands.

Several weeks later, when the thieves had recovered from their cuts, scratches, and wounds, they went back to work. They were determined to steal the pot of gold from the barber's house. They felt they deserved it for having plowed the earth, and they were bitter because Nabiha had mocked them on three occasions. At all costs, they wanted to recover their reputation as thieves.

So much time had gone by that the barber and his wife were convinced that the thieves had given up and would not bother them again. Summer was almost upon them, and since it was already quite warm outside, Nabiha had started to leave the bedroom window open at night. Because of this, the next time the thieves arrived, she heard them in the garden, coming up with a plan to get into the house. Determined to defend herself and her husband, Nabiha grabbed the largest knife they had and hid behind the door. When the first thief cracked opened the door and stuck his nose in, *swish!* Nabiha cut it off. The unlucky thief screamed loudly, his blood spreading everywhere.

"There's something sharp in here!" he cried to the rest of his crew. "I must have broken glass when I opened the door!"

Another thief tried to enter, certain that the glass had all been broken. But as soon as his nose appeared through the crack of the door, *swish!* Nabiha cut it off as well.

"Dear Allah!" screamed the second thief. "There's something sharp in here behind the door! It's ice-cold and made of metal! I must have crashed into a shutter and cut my nose!"

And so each thief tried in turn to enter through the door, each one failing after the other. Finally, only the leader of the thieves remained.

Looking around at his men, he came to a conclusion. "I won't open any door," he said. "I don't want to also end up wounded. Who would be left to watch over us then?"

And with that, the thieves left. Nabiha, thinking that she had saved herself, her husband, and their fortune, picked up the sliced-off noses and put them in a box.

What Nabiha hadn't considered was that a wounded thief isn't afraid when his pride is at stake. And so it was with these thieves, who had been defeated over and over: they weren't ready to give up yet. After allowing themselves to heal, they returned to the barber's house.

This time, the thieves arrived on a summer night so hot that Nabiha had put her bed in the garden, hoping that some gusts of wind would help her sleep. When the thieves saw Nabiha sleeping outside, they were confident they could outsmart her this time. Before they even started to look for the pot of gold coins, they hoisted her bed up onto their shoulders and brought it into the forest, where no one would hear her cries for help.

The motion woke Nabiha up, and in a few moments she understood what was happening; this time, she was scared for her life, with no way to escape. She stayed still so that her abductors wouldn't know she was awake, thinking.

"Let's stop here," the leader of the thieves suddenly said. "Put the bed between these trees so nobody sees us."

Thinking quickly, Nabiha stuffed her pillow under her blanket so the thieves would think she was still asleep, and then slipped out of bed and grabbed a nearby branch, pulling herself up into a tree.

As the thieves discussed who would be the lookout, Nabiha sat listening

from her perch overhead, all the while coming up with a means of escape. The thieves chose their leader to take first watch, after which the rest fell into a deep sleep.

It was time for Nabiha to put her plan into action. She hid her face behind her silky white nightgown and began to sing sweetly. Her song was so beautiful that the thieves' leader believed he was hearing a heavenly creature singing. He fell under the spell of the melody. Excited, he climbed to the branch where Nabiha was sitting. Since her face was hidden, she was sure he wouldn't recognize her.

"Oh, beautiful creature with such a heavenly voice," said the leader, "you have stolen the heart of the king of thieves."

"If you are the thief you claim to be, I can't believe a single word you say," answered Nabiha as sweetly as she could.

"What can I do, queen of the evening light, for you to believe me?" he asked, anxious to hear her response.

"Only if I can read the truth on your tongue will I know you are not lying," she answered.

Eagerly, the thief stuck out his tongue to be read, and *swish!* Nabiha cut it off. Bleeding profusely, the bewildered suitor fell from the branch to the ground, landing hard. He cried out, both from the pain in his heart and from the pain in his body. Startled by the thudding and the screams, the other thieves woke up, shocked to find their leader in such a state. Since he had no tongue, they couldn't understand his strange, babbling noises. Even so, they understood that Nabiha must have struck again.

As the band of thieves took the time to recover once more, they tried to devise another plan to get the gold they still felt they deserved for having plowed the earth. After much discussion, though, they reached the conclusion that Nabiha's intelligence was simply greater than theirs.

In a measure of last resort, they decided to consult the king in the hopes that he might come up with a solution. They presented their case to him, portraying themselves as the injured victims of Nabiha's cruel schemes. But he summoned the barber's wife to tell her side of the story, and Nabiha explained that all of her actions had been taken in self-defense. She then laid out her proof on the table, which was nothing other than the missing body parts of the thieves.

The king immediately saw the truth in what the woman had said, and locked up the thieves for a very long time. At last, Nabiha could rest and live her life in peace. From then on, people consulted with her and asked for her wise advice, which she gladly imparted with prudence and humility.

Katherine
Nutcracker

A Tale from Scotland

**P**rincess Caraderosa's mother died when she was a little girl, and she had no brothers or sisters. Though her father, the king, tried to spend as much time as possible with her, the demands of the kingdom kept him very busy, and so the princess was often alone. After much thought, the king grew determined to remarry so that his daughter would have company. He met a widowed countess with a daughter named Katherine who was the same age as the princess, and decided to marry the countess.

The two girls quickly grew to love each other. They spent all of their time together and considered themselves sisters. They shared everything, except for the love of the new queen, who considered the princess a rival to her daughter, especially since she was so pretty. Katherine loved animals, liked to jump and run around, and had no hesitation in doing tasks considered inappropriate for a young girl. Caraderosa, on the other hand, knew the arts and sciences, played the harp, and read astronomy books. She loved to hear visiting strangers talk about the customs in their own countries.

"No prince will ever be interested in Katherine," the queen lamented. "All the suitors will end up dazzled by Caraderosa."

One day, the queen asked a sorceress to take away the princess's beauty.

"Bring her to me tomorrow, before she's eaten anything, and I will turn her into such an ugly girl that she won't want to look at herself in the mirror," the sorceress replied.

So the queen suggested that Caraderosa go to her friend's house to try on a new dress.

"She's a great seamstress and has brought new cloth from the East," the queen said to her in an unusually cheery tone. "It would be best not to eat before you go, so you don't risk getting crumbs in the seamstress's cloth."

The princess, who had always known that her stepmother didn't love her, was suspicious of the queen's kind behavior. Not understanding why she had to fast, she went down to the kitchen and ate a slice of apple pie before leaving the palace. Then she went to the house of the sorceress, who was disguised as a traveling seamstress.

"Welcome, my beautiful Caraderosa," the sorceress said, draping her in a piece of silk cloth.

The cloth was supposed to cast a spell on Caraderosa. But when the sorceress placed it on the princess, the silk simply slid down to the floor and lost all its magical powers. The sorceress knew at once that the princess had not fasted that morning, for if she had, the silk cloth would not have fallen.

"Come back tomorrow, princess," the sorceress said, trying to hide her annoyance. "I will use the silk cloth to take your measurements again."

At the door, the sorceress asked the princess to deliver a message to the queen: "The songbird goes off pitch and cheeps if she eats grain."

Caraderosa didn't know what the message meant, but the queen understood at once: the princess had eaten something before going. She was determined to ensure that the same thing didn't happen again.

The next morning, a maid accompanied the young woman to the sorceress's home. The maid had been told that Caraderosa could not eat anything, and she succeeded in leaving the house with the princess not having taken a single bite. As they walked through the market, though, the princess saw grapes that were so juicy and bright that she couldn't stop herself from eating a whole bunch. Once again, when she got to the sorceress's house, the magical cloth fell off her body.

"Beautiful Caraderosa, I beg you to return tomorrow," the sorceress repeated. "I need to make a few more adjustments for the cloth to fit you."

She told the princess to give the queen the same message as the day before. Upon receiving it, the queen was so angry that she vowed to accompany the princess herself the next day, to make sure Caraderosa arrived at the sorceress's house without eating anything.

And so she did, and this time, when the sorceress draped the silk around Caraderosa, the bewitched cloth stuck to her body as if it were her own skin. It enveloped her from top to bottom, and transformed her head into that of a goat.

The queen laughed heartily, satisfied that she had finally succeeded. The sorceress disappeared, and the princess, horrified by her own looks, ran to hide in her chambers.

When Katherine learned what had happened, she became enraged by her mother's cruelty. She promised Caraderosa that she would do whatever she could to break the spell and that, in the meantime, she would stay with her so she wouldn't suffer because of her looks.

"Mother, if you've been cruel to my beloved sister, what else might you do?" Katherine asked the queen. "I won't stay another second in this castle—no one should have to live with the fear of being punished because of a whim."

Katherine covered Caraderosa's head with a shawl and they set off down the road to go as far away as possible. At sunset, they arrived at a farmhouse, and Katherine offered to brush the owner's horses in exchange for a meal and a place to sleep. The next day, after making their way down the road some more, they stopped at an inn and washed pots and pans in exchange for food and shelter. For several days they traveled in this way, until they reached the outskirts of the kingdom and crossed into the neighboring country.

Katherine wanted to see if she could get a job in the palace. "Wish me luck, sister," she said to Caraderosa. "It would be great if we could stay here. Not just a day or a night, but forever."

"That would be wonderful," Caraderosa wept. "But no one will hire you once they see my goat's head."

Katherine hugged her sister, trying to calm her. Thinking quickly, she devised a plan to explain why a shawl always covered her sister's head.

When they arrived at the palace, the royal butler greeted them. Seizing her chance, Katherine said, "I'm looking for a job, and I would be appreciative if you had any kind of work. The only request I would make is for my

sister, who has a strange illness that hurts her head, and who therefore needs lots of quiet. Might you have a job that I could do in exchange for rooms where my sister could rest peacefully?"

The butler listened carefully. Thinking that, since her sister needed peace and quiet, Katharine would know how to move around noiselessly, he had an idea. "The crown prince also suffers from a strange illness requiring silence," the butler said. "He is mostly sick at night—someone always needs to be with him. Be warned: taking care of him is so tiring that whoever does it ends up exhausted, but in exchange for the work, you and your sister could share a room tucked into a quiet corner of the palace. Perhaps you would be interested in this arrangement."

Katherine happily accepted the job, since it would allow her to be with her sister during the day. The butler set aside quarters for them, from which Caraderosa could gaze down upon the royal gardens without being seen.

"If the crown prince has a good night under your care," said the butler, "I will give you a small bag of silver coins as payment tomorrow morning." And with that, he left.

Katherine was pleased with the arrangement. Even if this job didn't last long, her sister would be able to spend at least one night in a bed and Katherine would be able to buy food for a few days with the coins she'd receive.

And so Katherine went to see the prince, who was handsome despite his pale skin and sickly demeanor. He stared blankly at the wall, stretching out his hands every once in a while as if there was something he wanted to touch. He kept this up for quite some time, until he fell asleep.

The night went on without any problems, until around midnight, when Katherine saw the prince growing restless. Close to dozing herself, Katherine shook herself awake and stared at the young man as he got up, dressed, and left his chambers. With Katherine following quietly behind, the prince walked down the stairs, a blank look on his face. Thinking that this behavior might have something to do with his illness, she continued to follow him.

The prince exited the palace and made his way to the stables, where he mounted a horse. Katherine climbed up onto a second horse, and the prince, still transfixed, didn't so much as notice. With Katherine still following a bit behind, the two riders galloped through the forest toward the flat plains. Along the way, Katherine had picked up a few nuts, thinking that it might be useful to have some food on hand, since she didn't know where they were going. Continuing to ride, the prince and Katherine crossed the plains, until the young man stopped his horse in front of a mound.

"Open up, small green mound," he whispered. "Let the prince and his horse enter."

Katherine didn't want to be left behind, so she also whispered: "Please let a lady and her steed enter as well."

The mound opened to reveal what was inside: the magnificent assembly hall of an amazing palace. The mound closed after they entered, yet they were in a place full of light, with dozens of candles and brilliant chandelier lamps lit.

Katherine glanced around, astonished. A lavish scene unfolded before her eyes: she saw luxurious curtains, golden chairs facing a burning fireplace, a richly carved table full of delicacies, and huge mirrors that reflected the gorgeous fairies and knights who were dancing a waltz in great harmony in the center of the hall.

It was undoubtedly the strangest, most magical place she had ever seen.

The fairies rushed up to the prince and insisted that he join the dancing. Looking more closely at him, Katherine noticed that the crown prince seemed happy and healthy, as if he had never been sick. She watched him dance with the fairies for the rest of the night, until a gong sounded and all the fairies disappeared.

The prince went back to his horse, ready to leave at once. The mound opened again and he rode out, galloping back toward the palace faster than he had come. And right behind, Katherine followed on her own horse.

Back in his chambers, the prince took off his clothes, lay down in his bed, and began to stare out blankly, as he had hours earlier.

In the morning, the butler came up to Katherine to ask her how the night had been. The young woman didn't dare mention the bewitched prince or the fairies in the palace, convinced that she would not be believed. She merely told the royal butler that the crown prince had had a good night, sunk in a deep sleep.

As agreed, the butler gave her a bag filled with silver coins in payment. The day passed by normally, and when night arrived again, Katherine resumed her post at the prince's bedside. Within hours, the events of the previous night repeated themselves. At midnight, the prince got dressed and left the palace, riding on horseback, followed by Katherine.

"Open up, small green mound; let the prince and his horse enter," he whispered when he reached the mound.

Katherine again added: "Please let a lady and her steed enter as well."

Inside the mound, Katherine went for a stroll. She encountered a small fairy with a tiny wand, humming to herself. "Swish, swish, swish. . . . Three strokes of this tiny wand will bring back Caraderosa's beauty," the fairy said.

Katherine felt her heart beating faster. It seemed like the fairy's chant could break her mother's spell! She looked through her pockets and found the nuts she had gathered from the forest the night before, then rolled them as if they were marbles until the little fairy noticed. Wanting to take part in the game, the fairy put down her wand, just as Katherine had thought she would. Katherine, seeing her opportunity, grabbed it. A few minutes later the gong sounded and, as had happened the previous night, Katherine and the prince rode their horses quickly to the palace.

Back in his chambers, once again the prince took off his clothes, lay down in bed, and stared out blankly. Not wanting to wait another minute, Katherine returned to her chambers, where her sister was in a deep sleep. She took the fairy's wand out and tapped Caraderosa's sad goat head three times. Instantly, Caraderosa's beautiful looks returned, just as the fairy had said.

When the butler spoke with her in the morning, Katherine told him that the prince had had another good night. She also said that her sister was cured, thanks to the good rest that the palace had afforded her.

"We would like to thank the king for his generous hospitality," Katherine added.

The king was so pleased by Katherine's care of his son that he wanted to give her gold instead of silver coins. "I would like you and your sister to be so comfortable among us that you won't ever leave," he said.

The two sisters accepted the king's generous hospitality, since Katherine wanted to continue taking care of the prince. She was committed to freeing him from what she now knew must be a spell he had been trapped under.

That night, as Katherine had predicted, the prince's routine repeated itself. At midnight, the young prince got dressed and left the palace on horseback, followed by Katherine.

"Open up, little green mound; let the prince and his horse enter," whispered the prince yet again when they reached the mound.

And Katherine again added: "Please let a lady and her steed enter as well."

Once more, the small mound opened and they entered the luxurious dance hall, where nothing had changed from the prior nights. Katherine sought out the tiny fairy, and she found her playing with an apple. Approaching the fairy, the young woman heard her sing: "Three bites of this apple and the prince will no longer be mad."

Katherine took out a few nuts from her pocket, thinking that the same game might work to distract the fairy a second time. But this night, the tiny fairy wasn't interested. Katherine, practical and determined as ever, cracked the nuts to reveal what was inside: beautiful and enticing golden fruits. The fairy, fascinated, forgot about the apple, and when the time came for the gong to sound and for them to leave, Katherine had the cure for the prince.

As soon as they reached the palace, the prince lay down on his bed and fell into a deep sleep. In the morning, when the butler came in to see how he had slept, Katherine asked him to bring the apple to the prince so he could smell it.

"That must be a delicious apple," the crown prince said suddenly.

Enthusiastically, Katherine cut a wedge, and the prince ate it with pleasure, though he was still out of sorts enough that he didn't see who had given it to him. His skin recovered the color of a healthy man's.

"I should eat more apple. It is most delicious," the prince exclaimed.

He took a second bite, again without noticing Katherine, and got out of bed, moving like the agile young man that he was. He walked over to the window. "I hope I can eat a bit more," he said, looking out at the garden. "This beautiful day has whetted my appetite."

At the third bite, the spell the prince had been under was fully lifted. He left his chambers and went down to the royal rose garden. There he found Caraderosa, talking cheerfully with his father about the virtues of a good king.

"Were you the one who saved me?" he asked the beautiful Caraderosa, still confused by what had happened.

"You have been saved by the same person who saved me," the princess replied. "My beloved sister, Katherine."

"I would like to meet her," said the prince. "I would have much to learn from someone intelligent enough to tell the difference between a spell and an illness."

Katherine came forward to meet the prince, and she told him how she had broken the spell. The young man, who saw how clever she had been to gather the nuts and to use them in creative ways, decided to name her Katherine Nutcracker.

Katherine realized that, as she had been caring for the prince, she had in fact also fallen in love with him. With the spell now broken, the prince discovered that he, too, had fallen in love. The prince and Katherine were soon married, and that is how Katherine Nutcracker became the new queen of that kingdom.

The Fish Girl

A Tale from France

Many years ago, a couple lived with their daughter in a very small house at the end of a river, near the sea. Aalis received anything she asked for, perhaps because she was an only child, or perhaps because her parents didn't know how else to raise her. Because she had everything she wanted, she didn't realize how lucky she was or how grateful she should be, and, worst of all, she felt no need to help others.

One day, when her mother was very tired, she asked her daughter to repair her father's fishing net, because he wanted to go fishing that night and the net was full of holes. As Aalis was terribly bored that afternoon and couldn't find anything better to do, she accepted her mother's request and went down to the water to work on the net. Though in the past she had often neglected her chores and gotten distracted by talking to anyone who approached her, now she discovered that she really enjoyed mending things, and so she devoted all her energy into repairing the net.

Just as she finished and was about to bring the net home, Aalis heard a splash behind her. Turning around, she saw a huge fish jumping in the air. She quickly cast the net into the water, and her throw was so accurate that she snared the fish.

"How beautiful!" exclaimed Aalis, looking at the fish's silvery sparkles.

"You should throw me back into the water," the fish said. "If you don't, I'll transform you into a fish."

Though Aalis was surprised to hear a fish talk, she did not want to let it go. Not only was it huge, it was the first fish she had ever caught, and she was determined to eat it that very night.

When she got home, she asked her mother to cook it. "It's a real shame that this fish talks," Aalis said. "But I want to eat it just the same. It's the first fish I've ever caught! Can you believe that it threatened to turn me into a fish if I didn't release it?"

Her mother tried to dissuade her from eating the fish. "You should throw it back into the water right away. Surely it's a magical creature, and if something happened to you, neither your father nor I could bear it."

Aalis laughed, convinced that nothing could hurt her. Besides, she was hungry, which had put her in a bad mood.

"I'm going to pick flowers for my hair," she said to her mother. "When I get back, I want my dinner ready."

Her mother relented and began cooking, and half an hour later, the fish was ready and smelled delicious. Aalis sat down at the table and picked up her fork, ready to eat.

As soon as the fish touched her lips, Aalis's body jolted. She felt terrible pain: her head seemed squashed, her eyes rolled side to side, and her arms and legs stuck to the sides of her body. She couldn't speak or breathe.

Aalis felt a strong urge to throw herself out through the window and into the ocean, and so she did just that. Immediately she felt better. She saw fish all around her and was confused about what had just happened. But at least, she reasoned, she hadn't died!

With that knowledge giving her strength, Aalis looked around at where she was. What was going on?

"Welcome to your new home," a fish said, swimming past her.

"Nonsense!" Aalis gasped, swallowing water. "I'm not a fish." After speaking, she swam to the surface so no one would see her cry.

"You disrespected a talking fish," another fish said, "and it had the power to make its threat come true. I know because we've all suffered the same fate. We all used to be humans and are now living our lives in the ocean as fish."

"A fish's life isn't so awful," added another fish. "Come, we will introduce you to the queen. She lives in a spectacularly beautiful palace."

Aalis had no desire to go with them, but she didn't want to stay alone either. So she swam after the other fish as they made their way to the palace. As they swam, Aalis looked around, astonished by the treasures appearing before her very eyes. She thought it was a shame that she had to be a fish to discover how wonderful life in the ocean could be.

She realized she knew little about the sea bottom. She had some vague knowledge of algae, and knew a bit about a few crustaceans and fish. But there was so much more down here than she could have ever imagined: magnificent coral reefs, pearls, amazingly gorgeous anemones, and other sea creatures so beautiful words could not describe them. She also saw some creatures that had never seen light, since they lived deep in the cracks of underwater rocks. Aalis was amazed to discover that there were also mountains at the bottom of the sea. At first, in the dim light under the sea, Aalis felt as if she were blind, but bit by bit her eyes grew used to the lower depths of darkness.

After a few hours, the small group of fish reached a very deep valley. Before her stood the palace of the queen of fish. It was definitely the most beautiful palace she had ever seen. The walls were made of pink coral, and strands of pearls framed the windows. Thousands of fish swam toward the assembly hall inside, where the queen received them. When it was her turn, Aalis saw that Her Majesty was a creature as strange as she was beautiful: half fish, half woman. She sat in a green-and-blue seashell, and she was breathtaking.

Aalis approached the queen and introduced herself nervously. When she was done telling the queen what had happened to her, the queen told her story.

"Long ago," she began, "I was also a young woman." The queen continued by explaining that her father had been the king of a large country. On the day she had been set to marry the prince of a neighboring kingdom, her mother had put a crown on her head and said that she would be not just a princess but a queen, unless she removed the crown.

She had a happy life and soon gave birth to a son, who became crown prince of the kingdom. She could not have been happier. But one day as she strolled through the royal gardens, a giant appeared and snapped away her crown. The giant gave the crown to his daughter and cast a spell over the prince so he could see no difference between his daughter and the queen. The prince, confused, professed his love for the giant's daughter.

The queen couldn't bear the change and, in a moment of despair, jumped into the sea. Her ladies-in-waiting, who loved her dearly, wanted to throw themselves into the sea as well, but a wizard who had seen everything took pity on them and wouldn't let them die. He transformed the queen and all of her ladies into fish, so they could live their lives out in the ocean.

"We will remain here, at the bottom of the sea, until someone recovers the crown and gives it back to me," the queen explained. And then she made a request: "Would you get it for me?"

The queen's story and her desire to return to land affected Aalis so much that she exclaimed: "Yes! Tell me what I must do."

Overjoyed, the queen began to tell Aalis how to find her crown. "You must go back to land and climb the mountain where the giant built his castle," she said. "You will find him crying after his daughter, who died while on a hunting trip with the prince. Before her last breath, she had a loyal servant return the crown to her father."

The queen assured Aalis that, if she followed her instructions, she would be perfectly safe. To help her on her mission, the queen gave Aalis the power to turn herself into whatever creature she wanted.

"Just touch your forehead and name the animal you wish to be," she explained.

With that, Aalis swam toward land. When she reached shore, she touched her forehead with her tail. "Stag, come to me," she said. Her small, watery body disappeared, and she transformed into a beautiful stag.

The stag took deep breaths, growing stronger by the second, and jumped across rocks and rivers. He ran all the way up the mountain, until he reached the castle where the giant lived. The walls were impenetrable, so he touched his forehead and became an ant, figuring this was the best way to enter unseen. The climb over the wall was difficult and tiring for this tiny insect. When she got to the top, she saw branches and transformed into a monkey. She swung from branch to branch until she reached the room where the giant slept.

Aalis wanted to talk to him, so she touched her forehead and became a parrot. A moment later, the giant awoke with a stretch and saw a beautiful pink bird.

"I've been sent to recover the crown," the parrot said. "It isn't yours anymore since the queen, your daughter, is dead."

Grief-stricken, the giant wailed, jumped from his bed toward the parrot, and tried to strangle her. Aalis flew away and escaped, and the giant realized he would be better off asking for something in exchange for the crown.

"Bring me a necklace of blue gemstones from the capital's San Martin Arch," he said to the parrot. "I will give you the crown for that."

Aalis agreed to this deal, and when the giant left her alone, she became an eagle. Perched on the windowsill, she felt her wings growing and strengthening, and she flew off toward the capital. When she reached the San Martin Arch, she used her beak to peck out the dirt around the gems. She loosened the stones and flew back to the giant.

"They aren't as blue as I had hoped," he growled, holding the gems in his large fingers. "I will have to ask you for something else, something equal to the value of the crown."

Aalis knew that the giant was trying to cheat her, but she had no choice other than to continue playing his game. This time, the giant asked for a crown of stars in exchange for the queen's crown.

Thinking hard, Aalis flew to a lake and turned herself into a frog. The stars glistened in the crystal-clear water as if they were really part of the sky. She gathered up the twinkling water and put it in a bag, then returned to the giant's castle. When she got there, she turned into a spider, then knitted a crown of fine threads, which she splashed with the water so that it would reflect the stars. When she offered it to the giant, he had no choice but to recognize Aalis's magical power.

"You have won fair and square," said the giant, giving her the crown. "Your powers are greater than mine."

Aalis became a parrot again and grabbed the queen's crown in her beak, flying off with it. As she traveled across the forest and back to the sea, she transformed herself into a monkey, then an ant, and finally, into a stag.

When she reached the seashore, Aalis stopped and cried, wanting to stay on the land. It was only when she remembered her promise to the fish queen that she turned back into a fish once again and returned to the underwater palace.

During her absence, the ladies who had been transformed into fish had lost hope of ever seeing Aalis again. So when she returned, they gathered around her happily, anxious to learn what had happened. They followed her all the way to the palace, where Aalis gave the crown to the queen. The moment she put it on her head, the queen regained her human form.

"You have succeeded!" she cried with joy.

While the queen thanked her, the other fish regained their human forms as well and swam back to land, filled with happiness.

They had been living so long at the bottom of the sea that they were surprised by all the changes they found ashore. The king had died, and the queen's son, who had been crown prince when they had left, now occupied the throne. When the queen appeared before him, her son could hardly believe his eyes, and he wept tears of joy as he embraced her. The queen told her son that he needed someone brave and with a noble heart to help protect the kingdom.

Aalis, whom the queen had taken on as an adviser since she had successfully retrieved the crown, was at the queen's side. The queen knew that Aalis would be worthy of the task.

"I want you, young Aalis, to help rule this magnificent kingdom," she said to her. "Having lived so many years under a magic spell has made me weary, and I don't have the strength to do it myself."

Aalis wanted to return home, see her parents again, and thank them for all they had given her. She now understood how self-centered and fickle she had acted when she had eaten the talking fish. Yet, thanks to the spell the fish had placed on her, she had discovered a courage she didn't know she had.

"Your Majesty, I am grateful for your confidence in me," Aalis said. "I hope to govern this land with the same wisdom you displayed when you ruled your kingdom under the sea."

The young woman asked the queen for permission for her parents live with her in the palace, so she could take care of them and could give them all the love they required.

This is how one of the bravest and most generous rulers of all time came to rule the kingdom.

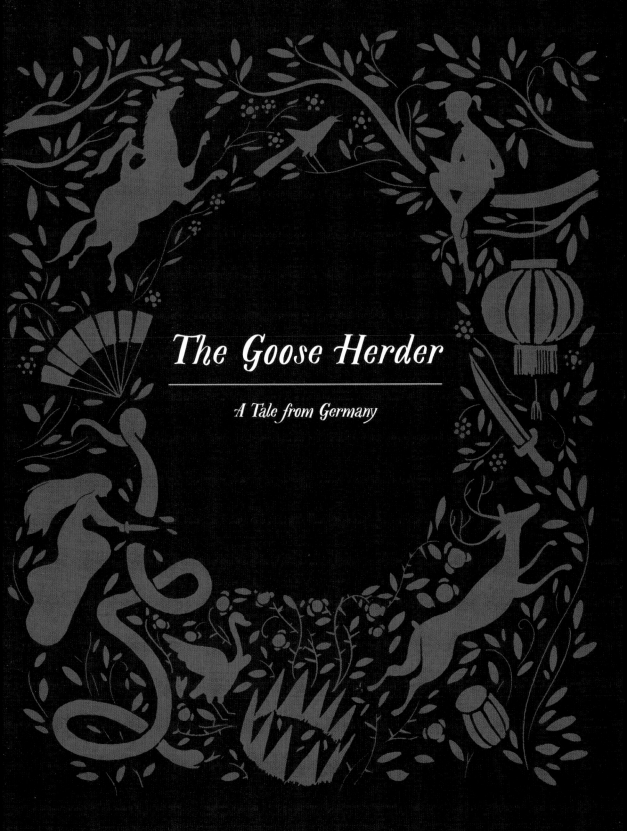

The Goose Herder

A Tale from Germany

nce upon a time, there was a king whose wife had died. Though he missed her, he didn't mind the solitude of not having a queen, since he felt enormously loved by his two daughters, whom he loved deeply as well. But the princesses were growing up, and he was afraid that soon they would stop loving and admiring him as much as they had when they were children. Tormented by this notion, he wanted to know how much they truly loved him.

One day when he could no longer contain his curiosity, he called his older daughter and asked her how much she loved him.

"Oh, Father, I love you so much," she answered. "There's no one in this world whom I could love more than you. I love you more than my very own eyes."

This answer pleased the king—to think that his daughter loved him as much as her own eyes was reason enough for his happiness.

Feeling satisfied, the king beckoned his younger daughter and asked her the same question.

"Oh, Father, I love you so much," she replied. "There's nothing in this world that I could love as much as you. Not only do I love you because you are my father, but I also love you for the courage in your heart, your generosity, and the wisdom of your actions."

"Tell me, dear girl, to what would you compare your love for me?" the king asked.

"There's nothing I love as much as you," she answered. "You are like the salt in all that I eat."

The king's face darkened; her answer disappointed him enormously. The fear of losing his daughter's love enraged him so much that he made an awful pronouncement.

"You must leave my palace before noon," he ordered. "I don't want someone near me who loves me like some spice. You are no longer my daughter!"

The princess felt a weight in her heart, a weight so heavy that it kept her from speaking. Her father's fury had robbed her of her voice, and she couldn't so much as find the words to explain what she had meant, nor could she apologize or let out the deep cry flooding her heart.

"Soldiers, take the princess far beyond the palace walls!" the king ordered. "She is forbidden to return. She is a stranger to me now and isn't welcome in my castle!"

With tears in her eyes, the princess went to her chambers, placed a few jewels and some clothing into a pack, and abandoned her home as fast as she could. When the castle gates closed behind her, she started walking aimlessly, not knowing where she was going. Without thinking, she found herself taking a path that led down to a riverbank.

When she was able to stop crying and regain some control over her heart, the princess began to think rationally again. The first thought that came to her was of how she would live—she only knew how to be a princess.

She played the lute beautifully, she embroidered with silk threads, and she knew her sciences and mathematics, but none of that would help her earn her keep. The next thought that crossed her mind was that she also had to hide her true identity, because any scoundrel could abduct her and try to get a huge ransom for her if they knew who she was. The memory of her father and the fear that he would not pay a ransom for her brought more tears to her eyes.

The princess went to the river to wash away her tears. Seeing the muddy bottom of the river gave her an idea. She rubbed dirt on her face to hide her delicate skin, smeared mud into her hair to hide its shine, and then tromped the damp earth with her bare feet. When she had finished, she was satisfied that nobody would suspect her noble lineage. She exchanged her elegant dress for a beggar's rags and ripped and smeared mud on her pack. Anyone who saw her would think she was a poor beggar without a crust of bread to eat.

And so the princess continued down the path she had started on. People gave her food and coins along the way, since she looked so needy, but she didn't want to spend her life begging. Several days went by in which she observed things she had never seen in the kingdom—farmers herding hogs and milking cows, shepherds shearing sheep, and workers tilling the earth. Her sense of discomfort grew and grew. She couldn't imagine how she would earn a living.

She continued wandering down the road and found herself passing through a village in a neighboring kingdom. There she saw an old woman, so frail that she was barely able to stand, herding geese to a trough of water. The princess hurried over to help her.

"I don't know who you are," the old woman said. "You aren't from around her, but I'm so tired and sick that your offer to help me is a blessing." The old woman looked into the princess's eyes and added: "I see a pure soul with no evil in your eyes. I know you won't steal my only means of support."

The princess helped the old woman to sit down and brought the geese to the trough. She helped her every day, slowly gaining not only the old woman's trust but also that of her neighbors, and after some time, the other villagers accepted her as one of their own. In addition to herding the geese, the princess baked bread for the village to earn her keep.

As time passed, the princess missed her home. To ease her sadness, she looked for a spot to bathe while the geese wandered near a river. Finding an ideal bend in the river, the princess submerged herself, and let the water clean her skin. Getting out of the river, she carefully combed her hair, remembering how her ladies-in-waiting had done it, and let it dry in the sun until it recovered its original shine. Then she put on one of the dresses that had been in her pack ever since she'd left the palace. Sure that no one could see her, she sat dressed on some rocks and gazed at her face reflected in the water.

That day, the son of the king from the neighboring kingdom went fox hunting and got separated from his group. Through the thick vegetation, he spied a young woman surrounded by geese, but was too far away to see her

clearly. Astonished by her elegance, he crept up close, trying to get a better view.

The princess, who sensed someone nearby, hurried off to disguise herself again. Though the prince tried to follow her, he tripped over some rocks and fell to the ground. By the time he got back up, she was gone. The princess took off her dress, put on her rags, and led the geese back to the village.

A short while later, the prince came into the village and asked after the beautiful goose herder.

"Dear sir, you must be mistaken," they told him. "Our goose herder is the hardest-working, most dedicated person in the village. She also makes the most delicious breads. But she is the dirtiest and ugliest woman anyone has ever seen."

The prince was confused by the answer. No matter how much he insisted, he got the same response, and after some time, he returned to his palace.

Days passed, but the prince could not forget the woman he had seen—he even lost his desire to eat. "What can we do to make you better?" asked his parents, not knowing what was weighing so heavily on his heart.

The prince was afraid that his parents would think less of him if he admitted to having fallen in love with a goose herder he had seen only once. So instead of offering a full explanation, he simply said, "Maybe I will get better if I eat bread from the nearby village."

Although they thought this was a strange request, his parents ordered their servants to bring the bread that the prince had requested.

When the servants came to the village and relayed the prince's request, the princess requested only flour, salt, and water. "All I ask is that you let me knead the dough alone," she added. "An order this special requires total silence."

When the princess was alone, she washed her hands carefully. Before beginning to knead the flour, salt, and water, she put on her rings, since she wanted her hands to be adorned with gems while preparing food for the royal table. When she had finished, she put away her rings, not noticing that one of them had slipped off a finger and gotten mixed in with the dough.

When the prince took a bite of the bread, he found the ring, which confirmed his suspicion about the goose herder. He had her called to the palace and, paying no attention to her rags, the prince showed the princess the ring.

"It's mine," the young woman answered, grateful that the prince had not judged her by her looks. "My dear mother, a queen in a nearby kingdom, gave it to me on her deathbed."

When the princess saw that the prince believed her, she knew there was no longer any sense in maintaining her disguise, and so she asked for a room where she could change her clothes.

When she returned to the prince's chambers minutes later in her regal dress, the prince was delighted, for at that moment he knew with certainty that she was the goose herder he had seen by the river.

The princess walked over to the prince and told him her story. Stirred by the sadness she had felt when her father repudiated her, the prince desired nothing more than for her to be happy again, and so he devised a plan.

Pretending that he intended to marry the princess, the prince invited her father to come to his kingdom for the wedding. As much time had passed since the princess had left home, the king regretted his unfair and cruel reaction and decided to go to his daughter at once, bringing his older daughter with him as well.

When the king saw the young princess, he hugged her with tears in his eyes. He knelt before her and begged her forgiveness for the cruel way he had treated her. His daughter forgave him at once, since she was so happy to be reunited with both him and her sister.

In that time, the ruse of a wedding between the prince and the princess fell by the wayside, and in its place, a real wedding was planned. For the princess had agreed to marry the prince, who had fallen in love with her even when he hadn't realized who she was. To celebrate the marriage, the princess asked that they serve her father bread made of just flour and water, a soup without salt, and meat and boiled vegetables without any spices.

The day of the wedding finally arrived, and the king's food was served. "Father, do you like your meal?" asked the princess, seeing that her father was hardly eating.

"Beloved daughter, the food looks delicious, but it's so tasteless that I can't eat it," her father confessed.

"Salt is an essential ingredient in cooking," the princess commented.

"Indeed that is so, my daughter," he replied.

"And yet you were offended when you asked me how much I loved you and I told you that you were as important to me as salt is to food," she recounted.

The king listened carefully to his daughter. He finally understood her and realized that he had been incapable of appreciating her wisdom.

But now, not only did he acknowledge his mistake, he also realized how much he admired her, since she had been able to chart her own future through her efforts and patience. Indeed she had, and her wisdom served her well through many years to come.

Anait

A Tale from Armenia

Many centuries ago, in the ancient kingdom of Armenia, the king's son, Vatchagan, went hunting with his servant, Nazar, and his dog, Zanzi. It was such a hot, humid day that they didn't catch sight of any prey, so Prince Vatchagan and loyal Nazar decided to visit the village of Atzik, where they would rest before returning to the palace. When they reached the central square, they were overwhelmed by the heat, so they sat by a fountain. Nearby, a group of young women had gathered around the water.

Very thirsty, the prince asked for some water. One of the young women dunked her jug in the fountain and brought up gleaming fresh water. But before the prince could bring the jug to his lips, one of her friends looked at the young man's tunic, which was soaked in sweat, and at his flushed face and dry lips, and pulled the jug away, spilling all the water on the ground. As the prince and his servant looked on with astonishment, the first young woman lowered her jug several times into the fountain and filled it with water, only for her friend to pour it out again.

"Why are you torturing me?" Vatchagan asked. "Do you want me to die of thirst?"

The friend observed the prince. Drops of sweat no longer ran down his face, and his breathing had returned to normal. She dunked her own jug into the fountain this time, and she offered it to him.

"We are a welcoming people," she answered. "We were simply waiting for you to recover a bit from the extreme heat. If you had drunk this very cold water when you were dying of thirst and soaked in sweat, you might have died. Now you are back to normal and can drink the water without fear."

The prince now understood what had been happening, and he was very impressed by how the young woman had responded. After engaging in further conversation, he discovered that her name was Anait, and that she was the daughter of Aran, a simple shepherd. Anait then wanted to know who he was and what his parents did.

But these were not questions Vatchagan wanted to answer, since he wished to remain anonymous.

"I'd like to tell you the truth, but I can't just yet," the prince replied.

And so Anait took her jug and went back home. The prince watched her leave, feeling despondent—he knew he had just fallen in love.

As time passed, Vatchagan grew sadder and sadder. He felt a weight in his heart; nothing could cheer him up. Finally, his mother asked why he was so very unhappy.

Deciding to be honest, he told her what had happened. "I would like to return to Atzik and marry Anait, the shepherd's daughter," he implored.

The king and queen refused to grant their son's request. The prince had to marry someone with royal blood, they said.

But Vatchagan refused to marry any other woman than Anait. He kept to his word for months, until his parents felt they had to investigate the young woman: they wanted to know what was so special about her, what had driven their son to fall so deeply in love. When they discovered she was a courageous and intelligent person, despite her humble roots, the king and queen gave in.

They sent loyal Nazar and two of their best advisers to Atzik to ask the shepherd for his daughter's hand in marriage. When the three men reached Aran's house, he greeted them as the great host that he was. Though poor, he offered them the few goods he had, and unrolled his best carpet in the center of the house so they could sit down. The beauty of that extraordinary room amazed Nazar and the advisers.

"What a gorgeous carpet," the visitors remarked. "Did your wife weave it?"

Aran explained that his wife had died ten years ago, and that Anait had woven the carpet. This news made Nazar and his two advisers very happy, for it was advantageous that the young woman the prince had fallen in love with was so talented.

"Your daughter has caught the attention of the royal family," said Nazar. "The king has sent us to summon her so that she may become the wife of the crown prince."

Aran listened but displayed no reaction. The king's emissaries had expected him to jump with happiness or thank the heavens, but he did no such thing. On the contrary, he stayed silent, carefully examining the carpet's patterns. Recognizing that he wasn't reacting in the way they anticipated, Aran knew that he would have to explain himself.

"I'm not the one who decides who my daughter will marry," he said. "Only she can decide something like that. If she is willing, you can count on my support. If she is unwilling, I will support her in her choice."

At that moment, Anait came into the room carrying a basket filled with apricots, dates, and nuts. She placed the basket on the table and sliced the fruit for the guests; then she went to her loom. The emissaries watched her, amazed, as she fluttered around her father's modest house. When she began weaving, her agile fingers moved with so much skill that they seemed to be interpreting a song on the loom.

Aran noted to the emissaries that Anait had taught many people in the village to weave.

"Why don't you have the people weave for you, Anait?" one of the emissaries asked. "You could become rich."

"They know how to weave," Anait answered, "but they prefer to work in the fields."

"You've also taught them to read and write," her father added.

It was true that the people of Atzik knew how to weave, read, and write, thanks to Anait. The forest trees surrounding the village had verses carved into their trunks. The stones in the river reflected beautiful words about life and water. On the village walls were phrases written in charcoal by the people. Thanks to Anait, this was a very cultured village.

"You should come to the palace, Anait," Nazar broke in, "and show our illiterate people how to read and write."

One of the emissaries presented the gifts sent by the prince to impress

Anait. Gorgeous silk dresses embroidered with gold threads, pearl necklaces, and emerald bracelets glistened in the darkness of the house. But Anait didn't seem interested.

"The crown prince wants you for his wife," Nazar added. "You would be our future queen."

Anait considered the offer. "Tell me," she asked, "does the prince have a profession?"

Loyal Nazar and the emissaries were surprised—the prince was, of course, the king's son, and he would one day inherit the crown. He had no need for a profession.

"Whether you are a prince or not," Anait went on, "you must have a trade.

"Take away all these gifts," she added. "Please ask the king to forgive me, but ever since I was a little girl, I knew I wouldn't marry a man who didn't have a trade."

There was so much determination in Anait's words that the visitors simply left. When the king and the queen learned of the country girl's response, they felt relieved: they had suspected that they would never be entirely happy with a marriage between their son and Anait, and now it seemed they would no longer have to feign joy for their son.

Vatchagan, however, had a different reaction. "Anait is right," he said. "I should have a profession like everyone else. The fact that I'm a prince is no excuse."

The crown prince's answer displeased the king, who thought that being a prince should be enough for his son. But seeing that his son was set on finding a profession, the king brought together all his advisers and, after much discussion, determined that a warrior was the most appropriate profession for a prince. But Vatchagan ignored their counsel—he knew he needed a more useful trade for everyday life. And so, thinking of Anait, he chose to learn the art of weaving.

The king, seeing that his son was set on this goal, instructed his advisers to seek out the most skilled artisan in all the kingdom and, within the year, Vatchagan had become an exquisite weaver. His first task, he knew, was to weave a beautiful carpet for Anait. When he had finished, one of his emissaries brought it to her.

Upon receiving Vatchagan's gift, the young woman said, "Bring this carpet that I have woven back to the prince. I accept his proposal of marriage."

The two soon wed, and a period of harmony and abundance followed. A few years later, Vatchagan inherited the crown, and he and Anait became king and queen.

One day, Nazar, Vatchagan's loyal servant, disappeared. The royal pair commanded their subjects to search for him throughout the kingdom, but to no avail: it was as if the earth had swallowed him whole.

All the while, the kingdom continued to prosper and the people lived in peace and contentment. Anait wanted to make sure that no subject was unhappy, and she also wanted to focus her husband's mind on something other than Nazar.

"Perhaps you should leave the palace and walk among the people," Anait suggested to Vatchagan. "You can teach them your skill so that more people will know how to weave. This way you will find out if your subjects are truly happy."

The king, who hadn't gone hunting for some time, realized that he hardly ever left the palace anymore. He praised his wife's wisdom, and the next day, he began his trip.

"Don't worry, I will govern in your absence," the young queen said.

"I'm not worried," the king answered. "On the contrary, I couldn't be leaving my kingdom in better hands."

Anait and Vatchagan said goodbye to each other. He warned her that if he didn't return within ninety days, or if she didn't receive news from him, it was because he either was in danger or had been killed.

Thus, the young king set out on his way.

After a few weeks of enjoyable travel, Vatchagan came to the city of Perodj. There, he was assaulted by a band of thieves who, not recognizing who he was, stole his money, took his clothes, and threw him into a hidden rocky cave.

"Tell us what you can do," said the leader. "If you have a skill, we will let you live. Otherwise . . ." And he dragged his thumb across his neck as if it were a knife.

"I can weave cloth more valuable than if the threads were made of gold," Vatchagan responded.

The thieves didn't believe him; they thought that maybe the poor man was lying to save his skin. Yet, they reasoned, nothing would be lost if he were to weave some cloth to be sold in the market.

"You'd be better off weaving something truly valuable," the leader growled, but he gave orders for Vatchagan to be sent to the back of the cave to begin his work in any case.

At the back of the cave was an enormous room, full of cracks and dampness and many men at work. When Vatchagan got to his spot, the thieves ordered him to sit on the ground and start weaving immediately.

And so he did, for several days. There was no sunlight, and he had nothing to eat or drink; all he did was work under the light of a squalid candle.

One day, when there were few guards about, Vatchagan decided to explore the cave, thinking that he might find a way out. After making his way through several tunnels, he was shocked to find his loyal servant, Nazar, who was so weak and exhausted that he didn't so much as speak for fear that his weak heart would give out.

With renewed determination and a plan forming in his mind, Vatchagan returned to his place and continued to weave.

When the thieves came back, they inspected his work. "Have you finished weaving yet, you scoundrel?" one of them bellowed. "Give me the cloth right now. I want to bring it to the market and see if it is worth as much as you say."

"Oh, it is worth more than you can imagine," Vatchagan answered. "Actually, you won't find a buyer at the market to pay in gold what it's worth."

"So what good is it?" roared the thief.

"You can get a huge amount of money for it," Vatchagan explained. "Just show it to Queen Anait. She knows the true worth of the cloth and would pay a good sum for what I've just woven."

Once again, the leader of the thieves realized that he would lose nothing if he were to try what his prisoner suggested.

He went straight to the palace. It was easy for him to get an audience with the queen, who was so worried by the king's prolonged absence that she would meet with anyone who might have a clue as to where he was.

The thief entered the royal halls posing as a merchant and showed her the golden cloth carefully folded on a marble tray. As soon as she saw the exquisite embroidery, the queen knew that it had to have come from her beloved. As she considered how to coax more information out of the man without revealing that she was asking about the king's whereabouts, something in the beautifully woven cloth caught her eye.

The queen unfolded the cloth and carefully examined it. She noticed a message hidden within the magnificent pattern and realized that her husband had crafted it so that no one but her could see it.

My loveliest Anait, it read, *I have been taken prisoner. The man bringing you this cloth is a ruthless thief who has imprisoned me and dozens of other unfortunate people. Nazar is also being held here. Search for us east of the city of Perodj, inside a cave hidden by huge boulders, near a lake shaped like a half-moon. Make haste, or we may all die soon. Vatchagan.*

"My dear merchant," said Anait, trying to hide her relief at having found this message, "this cloth has a beauty only I can appreciate. Tell me, where did you find such a lovely piece?"

The thief, who wasn't prepared for this question, attempted an explanation, but instead tangled up all his words. The queen didn't need to obtain any information from him, though, for her husband had provided all that she needed. Not wanting to lose another minute, she jailed the thief and gathered her army.

"Soldiers, our king is in captivity near Perodj. Let's go rescue him!"

Leading the soldiers, Anait set off on the road to the city where their king was imprisoned. They rode on horseback without resting until they reached the lake shaped like a half-moon. Near it, they found the entrance to a cave hidden between two enormous boulders. There was an iron gate at the entrance, which the soldiers easily knocked down.

With Anait leading the charge, the soldiers entered the cave in droves, using torches to find Vatchagan. The queen's eyes roamed over the countless prisoners trapped in the cave, and in a firm, kind voice, she instilled courage and trust in the captives.

"I am your queen, Anait," she said. "Don't worry, your suffering will soon end. We have come to save you."

With those words, Anait's voice reached Vatchagan and Nazar. The king gathered his remaining strength and came forward to meet his wife. After embracing and thanking the heavens for their lives, they went to find Nazar.

"My queen, today you have saved us," the servant babbled, before bursting into tears.

"You have saved us twice," said Vatchagan, looking lovingly into his wife's eyes. "Once today, but also when you asked years ago if the king's son had a profession."

The king returned home with his queen and loyal servant, and order was restored. The thieves were executed for their cruelty, and the prisoners recovered their health and were reunited with their families. Nazar, now old, stopped serving the king but remained his close friend. Together, Vatchagan and Anait governed the richest and most just kingdom of all time. And to this day, centuries later, people recall the legend of this queen, who knew how to rule her kingdom with her unique wisdom.

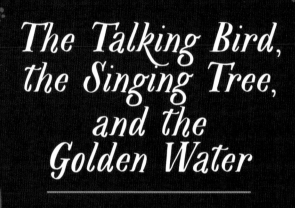

The Talking Bird, the Singing Tree, and the Golden Water

A Persian Tale from
One Thousand and One Nights

Hundreds of years ago, the sultan of Persia fell in love with a commoner. This young woman was both careful and considerate, and when she married the sultan, she was taught to behave like a true queen by her ladies-in-waiting. Despite her humble and simple nature, the queen's good fortune awakened the jealousy of her two sisters, who were selfish and without scruples.

Waiting patiently for the right moment, like animals eyeing their prey, the queen's sisters plotted to turn her happiness into suffering. So when the queen became pregnant, the sisters realized their moment was near. The day the queen gave birth, the two sisters stole her baby before she had even seen him, put him in a wicker basket, and threw him into the Aras River. They then told the sultan that his wife had given birth to a cat.

The Aras waters carried the newborn to the estate of a rich merchant. The man had not found a wife with whom he could share his life, but still he wanted an heir. When he saw the baby in the basket, he took it out of the water and thanked Allah for having answered his prayers.

The sultan and his wife were so sad that they went into mourning. It was only when the queen once more became pregnant a year later that happiness returned to their hearts. But their happiness was short-lived, as the queen's cruel sisters once again carried out the same devious plan as they had with the firstborn, sending this second baby down the river as well.

"Your wife has brought another cat into the world," they lied again to the sultan.

The sultan grew dispirited. He couldn't believe his terrible misfortune. He and his wife hugged, giving each other the strength to face their loss together.

Once again, the nearby merchant found a basket floating down the Aras River and, remembering what he had found inside the last basket, he hurried to pick it up. Though he hadn't dared to hope for his luck to repeat itself, he couldn't contain his happiness when he looked inside the basket and once again saw a small bundle. Just as with the first baby, the merchant brought this one home and raised him as if he were his own child. He named the two boys Farid and Faruz.

Three years into their marriage, the sultan's wife conceived a third child. She gave birth to a daughter, but even this didn't derail the plans of the queen's heartless sisters, who once more abandoned the baby on the waters of the Aras River.

"Your wife, kindly sultan, has given birth to a third cat," the sisters continued their lie. "We pity your misfortune."

This time, the sultan blamed his wife. Consumed by the pain of losing her third child without so much as seeing her, and never imagining that her sisters would trick her, the queen decided to devote her life to Allah and prayer. And once again, the merchant plucked the basket out of the water, knowing by now what he would find inside. He was especially happy to have a daughter under his roof. He decided to name her Farizad.

The three siblings grew up lacking nothing. They had the love of a father who was devoted to them; they studied astronomy, law, poetry, and alchemy; they rode horses and hunted. They learned to dance and play the noble game of chess. They were taught to trust family and to have moral principles, both of which made their father proud.

Time went by, and the merchant became an old man; and so it came to be that he passed away without having ever revealed to his children the truth of where they'd come from.

One day when Farizad was alone in the house, a traveler came along, looking for a place to say her prayers. The sultan's daughter offered her a beautiful spot in the garden and showered her with attention. Before the traveler left and went on her way, she spoke to Farizad.

"This is a magnificent estate," the woman said. "It's been a long time since I've seen such a beautiful place. But there's no happiness here. Something is missing."

"What's missing, my good woman?" asked Farizad.

The woman replied, "A talking bird, a singing tree, and golden water, from which a single drop could produce an endless fountain of gold."

The very notion of those three things sounded wonderful to Farizad. If she could only procure them for her family, they would have such happiness!

"Tell me more about these treasures," she requested. "I want to learn everything."

The traveler explained that Farizad could find all three things together in one place, within the confines of the kingdom. All she had to do was travel east for twenty days without straying from the path, until she reached the house of a pious dervish.

"On the twentieth day, you will meet an old man, the dervish," the traveler said. "He will tell you how to bring back the three treasures." And with that, she left.

Farizad waited impatiently for her brothers to return so that she could tell them what she'd learned. When they came back, she explained what had happened, and Farid, wanting to provide such happiness for his siblings, gathered his things so that he could set off at once.

"I will bring back the talking bird, the singing tree, and the golden water," he said before leaving. Then, to prevent Farizad from worrying about him, he continued, "Sister, please take this dagger. Look at its glistening blade every so often. If you notice that it is losing its glow and dripping blood, you can be certain that something has happened to me. Only then should you shed tears."

After a final embrace, Farid got on his horse and said goodbye to his siblings. He traveled across Persia without stopping to rest, and on the twentieth day, he found an old man blocking his path. It was the dervish Farid had expected, a man dedicated to a life of meditation; when the dervish opened his eyes, Farid went up to him.

"Good man," said Farid, "I am looking for the bird that speaks, the tree that sings, and the golden water. A traveler told my sister that you knew where they could be found."

The old man took a deep breath, held it in his lungs, and slowly let it out before answering. "Young man, I know where they are," he began. "I also know the dangers that looking for them entails—you aren't the first person who has come to ask me for these three treasures. No one who has gone looking for them has returned. If you would like an old man's advice, I suggest you go back and forget this mission."

"I'm not afraid of anything," Farid answered. "If these treasures bring happiness, I must bring them home."

The dervish insisted no further, realizing it was fruitless to argue. He breathed again and closed his eyes before answering; it was as if he were seeing a map in his mind.

"Take this ball," the old man said. "Roll it and follow until it finally stops at the foot of a mountain. Get off your horse and climb the mountain. As you go up, you will see many black rocks and hear a medley of voices. Don't listen, because they will be shouting insults and curses to try to get you to turn back. And don't look back either; if you do so, you will be transformed into a black rock. You'll see many such rocks along the way—each is someone who attempted to climb the mountain and failed. When you get to the top, you will find a cage with a talking bird. He will tell you where the tree that sings and the golden water are."

"Is that it?" the young man asked, thinking that the task didn't seem as difficult as he had feared.

"That's it. Do what you must do, and may Allah be with you," said the dervish. And he began meditating so deeply that he didn't even notice when the young man left.

Farid set the ball rolling just as the old man had instructed. He followed it on horseback until it stopped at the foot of a mountain. There, he got off the horse and began climbing to the top. As he went, he saw the black rocks that the dervish had described and began hearing the voices growing louder and louder, insulting and threatening him. Farid tried to ignore them and kept on climbing, but the insults were so offensive that he glanced back, hoping to gain solace from the quiet rocks. As soon as he turned around, he became a rock as black as the others.

At that very moment, across the kingdom, Farid's sister saw a drop of blood dripping from the dagger's blade. She knew at once that her older brother had encountered a terrible misfortune. She and Faruz wept sadly for their missing brother.

A few days later, Faruz announced that he was leaving. "I want to find out what happened to our brother," he said. "I will praise Allah if I find him safe and sound, but if he is dead, I will avenge his death."

Farizad tried vainly to dissuade him.

"I will leave you my beaded necklace," he told her. "It has one hundred pearls. Shake them every day, and as long as they keep moving, don't worry about me. Only if the pearls stick should you weep for me."

Then Faruz got on his horse and went down the road that his brother had taken all those days earlier His sister stood quietly, not moving until she saw him disappear over the horizon.

On the twentieth day, Faruz met the same dervish, who behaved and spoke exactly as he had with Faruz's brother.

"Do what you must do," he repeated, before returning to his meditations. "And may Allah be with you."

Faruz took the ball from the old man and let it roll on the ground. He dug his spurs into his horse to follow the ball, which stopped at the foot of the very same mountain. Faruz started climbing up to the top. He ignored the black rocks that crossed his path. But when he heard the very first insult, he took out his sword and turned around to face his enemy. He had forgotten the dervish's warning and was transformed into a black rock like all the others.

At that moment, far from there, the pearls stopped moving in his sister's hands, and Farizad knew something had befallen Faruz.

Alone and sad, Farizad knew she had to follow in her older brothers' footsteps. She saddled her horse for the long journey. After twenty days on horseback, she stopped in front of the dervish. He repeated the same words he had said to so many others before. He noted that Farizad was the first woman to try to get the three treasures, but he didn't think that would help her at all. The outcome, he was convinced, would be the same.

Before continuing on her journey, Farizad thought about how she could ignore the voices, which she knew would be the biggest challenge. She decided to make earplugs out of cloth and put them in her ears. After doing that, she thanked the dervish for his help and rolled the ball. Farizad followed the ball to the foot of the mountain, and when it stopped rolling, she dismounted from her horse and began to climb. Soon she heard voices penetrating her earplugs. But she refused to pay attention to the insults and curses—she didn't want to be scared by the threats and glance back.

To avoid temptation, she began to sing; hearing her own voice calmed her fears, and she was even able to remove her earplugs. In this way, she managed to avoid the fate of her two brothers.

When she reached the mountaintop, the first thing she saw was a beautifully carved, magnificent cage with a resplendent bird inside. She came close, watched the bird, and then, with amazement in her voice, asked where she could find the golden water.

"Walk to the north and you will find it," the bird answered.

Farizad started walking. She soon came to a spring that spouted water the color of amber against the light. She came nearer and stuck her hand in the water. It was the golden water the traveler had mentioned. She poured some of the water into her goatskin and returned to the talking bird.

"Most beautiful bird: Where can I find the tree that sings?" she asked.

The bird said that it was in the middle of the forest. "You only need one shoot from the tree," he explained. "Plant it in your garden when you get back, and it will grow with the same powers of the tree from which it was taken."

Farizad went into the forest. When she began to hear a beautiful tune, she followed it to the leafiest, most spectacular tree she had ever seen. A soft breeze caressed the leaves, producing an enchanting sound. Following the talking bird's instructions, she cut off a shoot, and then returned to his perch once again.

Before Farizad started her climb back down the mountain, she picked up the cage and asked the bird one last question. "My brothers are here, changed into black rocks," she lamented. "Tell me, pretty bird, how can I save them?"

"Sprinkle a drop of golden water on each rock, and whoever is there will come back to life," said the talking bird.

She followed the bird's instructions to the letter. As she went down the mountainside with the goatskin, the tree shoot, and the caged bird, she sprinkled drops of water on the rocks. When the magical water touched each rock, the spell broke and a grateful knight appeared, each one thanking her profusely.

And so Farizad saved everyone who had attempted but failed what she had tried and succeeded at, including her two brothers, who hugged and kissed her with joy.

The three siblings returned home with the treasures Farizad had obtained, and with all the knights she had saved. In his new home, the bird talked with anyone who came near; the music from the tree could be heard beyond the walls of the estate; and the fountain into which she had poured the golden water flowed on and on. The nightingales and the meadowlarks who lived nearby fluttered around, watching all the transformations with astonishment.

Soon it was known throughout the kingdom that there were three amazing treasures in the merchant's old estate. When the sultan heard this, he wanted to see them with his own eyes and announced his visit to the newly famous house.

Farizad asked the talking bird what she could offer the sultan, since she had never had a royal visitor come.

"Prepare a lavash, a thin unleavened flatbread, with the finest flour that you have. When you fold the bread over, fill it with pearls," the bird answered.

Farizad thought this was a very strange suggestion, but the talking bird had helped her so many times before, so she did exactly as he had instructed. She bought a small jewelry box filled with beautiful pearls and placed the gems very carefully in the center of the lavash.

When the sultan came to their house, he was pleased by the cleverness of the three siblings. He praised the house, enjoying the garden and the amazing fountain of golden water.

Farizad invited him to hear the tree that sang.

The sultan could hardly believe his ears. "Do you have a group of musicians living inside this amazing tree?" he asked. "Are the instruments playing these melodies under the ground, perhaps?"

Instead of answering, Farizad brought the sultan to meet the talking bird.

"Welcome, Sultan of Persia," said the bird, spreading its beautiful wings. "May Allah shower you with happiness."

The sultan was astonished by what he had seen and heard. This was truly a magical place. Moreover, he felt a strange peace in the presence of the three young siblings, even though they were unknown to him.

After seeing the talking bird, the sultan sat at the table together with his hosts, who honored him with a feast of dates, nuts, and honey. He was impressed by the fine texture of the lavash. His astonishment increased when he opened the bread and found real pearls inside.

"Are you surprised to see a lavash filled with pearls, Your Majesty?" asked the bird. "Why should this surprise you, when you weren't surprised that your wife gave birth to three cats?"

The sultan grew sad remembering.

"That's what my sisters-in-law assured me," he responded.

The bird then revealed what none of them had known: he told the sultan about how the queen's sisters, consumed with jealousy, had deceived him. He spoke of the great love that the merchant had given to the three babies the sultan's sisters-in-law had cast into the Aras River, and about the magnificent education that he had provided them with.

"If you have been delighted by this fabulous house, you will be further delighted to know that this is where your three children, two boys and a girl, were raised," the bird said. "Your children are none other than Farid, Faruz, and Farizad, the three young people who have opened the doors of this house to you."

The sultan felt burning tears running down his cheeks. He knelt on the ground and asked his children for forgiveness for having believed such evil lies. The children hugged the sultan, not forgetting the love given to them by the man who had cared for them and fed them until his death.

The sultan went to the queen to ask for her forgiveness, and also to bring her to meet her three children. When she arrived at their home, she recognized the three siblings the moment she laid eyes on them. And so it was that Farizad's courage and determination brought happiness to her entire family, which was finally reunited after all those years.

Myriam Sayalero is a journalist and the director of the multiplatform content site Adosaguas. She has had several books published in Spain and Mexico. The most recent are *Los regalos de la vida* (Aguilar, 2016), *Diario irreverente del desamor* (Planeta México, 2017), and *Poderosas* (Larousse México, 2017). Her latest children's publications are *¡Vaya con el día especial!* (Alfaguara, 2017) and *Diario de emociones* (Larousse, 2017).

You can visit Myriam online at
myriamsayalero.com
or follow her on Twitter
@myriam_sayalero

Dani Torrent has a degree in art history from the University of Barcelona and studied fine arts and illustration at the Llotja Advanced School of Art and Design. He has exhibited his award-winning artwork around the world, and has been published in many countries. In addition to his work as an illustrator, he has also written several of his own books in Spanish. He has won the Young Creators prize of the Fita Foundation of Girona (Spain), the second-place prize of the international drawing festival of Zabrze (Poland), and the second-place prize of the BIISA Festival of Amarante (Portugal). Dani lives in Barcelona.

You can visit Dani online at
danitorrent.com
or follow him on Twitter
@danitorrent1

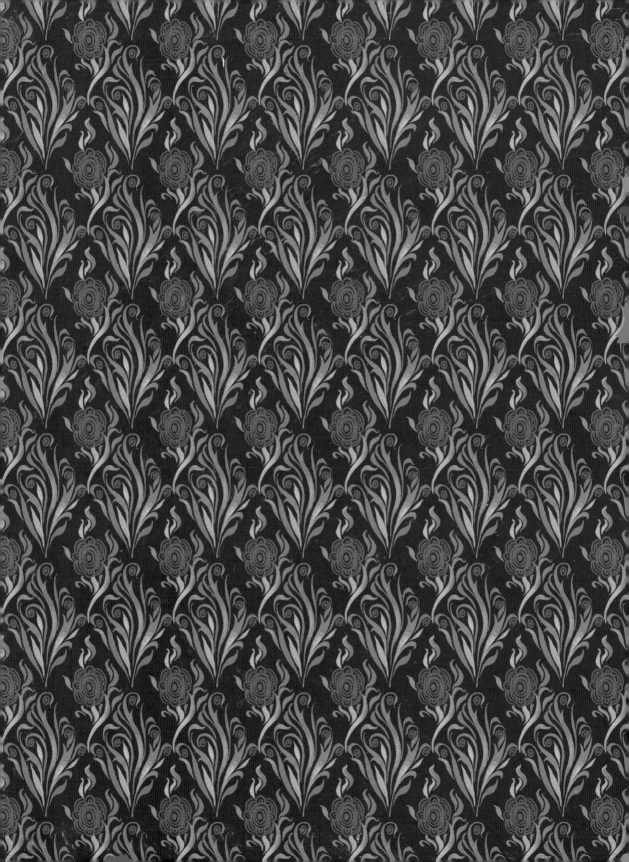